"Emily...Emily, what did I do?"

"You made me fall in love with you! And now you've come back and stirred everything up again!"

Gabe was shocked. He'd never seen Emily cry like this. She obviously wanted children very much. And it was *his* fault she didn't have any. He felt helpless with guilt and regret. He picked up the donor catalog, imagining Emily making a selection and then going through the unemotional procedure alone.

"Oh, Em. Don't do this."

"This isn't a whim of mine, Gabe. I've been preparing for over a year. I'm ready to have a child," she said simply.

And he heard himself say, "Then let me give you one."

Dear Reader,

When you were growing up, did you and your best friend decide to have your children at the same time so they could also be best friends? I did—which is how I got the idea to write my new couplet PROJECT: PREGNANCY.

But life got in the way for us, as it does for Emily and her best friend Freddie. We put off having babies to have a career, but when we were ready for babies, we were *ready*—and Emily and Freddie are now *ready!*

Writing about their pregnancy adventures reminded me of my own and so, naturally, I had to go upstairs and look in on my own baby boys...who promptly informed me that they are no longer babies and made me take all the stuffed animals out of their rooms!

I hope you enjoy the two PROJECT: PREGNANCY stories. As for me, I now have stuffed animals living in my office!

Love,

Heather MacAllister

Look out for Freddie's story
The Motherhood Campaign
in November 2000 (#3629)

THE PATERNITY PLAN
Heather MacAllister

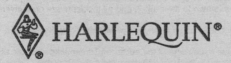

TORONTO • NEW YORK • LONDON
AMSTERDAM • PARIS • SYDNEY • HAMBURG
STOCKHOLM • ATHENS • TOKYO • MILAN • MADRID
PRAGUE • WARSAW • BUDAPEST • AUCKLAND

To Marie Monk Samp
with Alpha Gam love

ISBN 0-373-03625-6

THE PATERNITY PLAN

First North American Publication 2000.

Copyright © 2000 by Heather MacAllister.

PROLOGUE

"IF MY brand-new husband doesn't get back here with the rum dingers soon, I'm going to think the honeymoon is over." Emily Shaw, or rather Emily *Valera* now, peered over the top of her sunglasses and scanned the path leading from the row of quaint thatched-roof cabins to the resort lodge.

"Don't worry. I'll send *my* brand-new husband after him." Freddie, Emily's best friend and fellow bride, patted the bronzed shoulder of the man sleeping on the chair next to her.

Emily shook her head and held her finger to her lips.

Freddie grinned. "Lounging around on our own private beach with handsome men at our beck and call day *and* night...this is the life we were meant to lead, right, Em?"

"Hmm." Emily scooped a handful of white, powdery sand and watched it sift through her fingers onto the row of paper umbrellas she and her friend, Freddie, had stuck between their lounge chairs.

Actually the life she was meant to lead involved the pitter-patter of tiny feet and the sooner, the better as far as Emily was concerned.

Freddie disagreed. And ever since they were children, when Freddie and Emily disagreed, it was usually Freddie who prevailed.

5

But not this time.

Freddie could put off having babies for a while if that's what she wanted, but Emily, an only child, hungered for children of her own. Lots of children. And she'd found the perfect father in Gabe Valera. They'd have his dark, curly hair and maybe his brown eyes as well. Gabe, being a botanist, would be able to chart out the genetic possibilities—and probably would.

Emily smiled to herself. She knew that according to the grand life plan she and Freddie had plotted, they were supposed to establish themselves in their careers before they had children. And then they'd have them at the same time, so their children could grow up being the best friends she and Freddie were.

Except that Emily didn't want to wait to have children until she'd established a fast-track career. What would be the point of that? Right now the only track she wanted to be on was the mommy track. Besides, Gabe was so ambitious, he'd have enough career for both of them.

And now Freddie was even talking about going to law school. More school? Not for Emily. They'd just *graduated*, for Pete's sake. They'd just gotten *married*. Law school wasn't in the plan. Just because Hunter, Freddie's husband, was going to law school...

And speaking of husbands—where *was* Gabe? She twisted around to look down the path again.

"Instead of sending Gabe to the lodge, why didn't you call Aldo?" Freddie asked and stretched. "I tipped him enough so he should come running the next time we ring for him.''

"Gabe and I didn't like Aldo ogling you two," rumbled a low voice from the lounge chair on the other side of Freddie. "We had a little chat with him and he suddenly remembered pressing business elsewhere.''

"Oh, Hunter, you didn't!" Freddie laughingly protested.

"I didn't." Hunter Cole raised his head and smiled lazily. "But we tipped him more than you."

The passionately possessive look he gave her friend tugged at something within Emily. She pretended to rearrange the paper umbrella collection so she wouldn't have to witness the inevitable kiss that followed.

Gabe doesn't look at you like that.

Of course he didn't, and Emily didn't want him to. Hunter was a little too possessive of Freddie, in Emily's opinion. *She* wouldn't like it, and she wasn't nearly as independent as Freddie was. But to each her own, which was why Emily had married the intensely brilliant and charming Gabriel Valera, and Freddie had married the equally brilliant and quietly driven Hunter Cole in a glorious double wedding five days earlier.

And in spite of being a tad thirsty, Emily was happy. Fabulously happy.

The kiss continued.

Not that she couldn't be happier. "Since our jealous husbands ran off Aldo, I hope Gabe remembers to ask for extra fruit garnish,'' she said with forced brightness.

Pulling away from her husband, Freddie laughed. ''If it weren't for the fruit, we'd be living on love alone.''

''Speaking of...'' Hunter trailed off suggestively.

Freddie and Hunter exchanged another look before both rose to their feet, linked arms around each others' waists, and headed to their beach cabin.

Emily's face grew warm and it had nothing to do with the temperature on the beach at St. Thomas. It didn't have anything to do with being embarrassed, either. It was just that she'd been married only five days and...where *was* her husband?

Emily peeled herself off the towel-covered lounge chair and massaged the tiny terry-cloth dimples impressed on the back of her thighs. Towel dimples always took a long time to fade. Shrugging into her cover-up, she brushed at the sand that clung to her feet, slipped on her beach thongs and headed up the grass-lined path toward the main lodge.

Emily didn't expect to make it all the way to the lodge without encountering Gabe, but he was nowhere in sight.

She stepped into the lobby and blinked until her eyes adjusted from the bright sun. The rickety hotel bus had just arrived and disgorged several couples who were toting their luggage to the reception area. Emily skirted around them toward the bar, but there was no sign of Gabe.

Walking around the tiled fountain, Emily spied the gift shop. She smiled. Gabe must be renting snorkel equipment. He knew how she loved snorkeling.

Pushing aside the strings of shells hanging in the doorway, Emily stuck her head inside the gift shop. He wasn't in there, either.

It was possible that she'd missed him on the way back to their cabin, but the four of them had quickly discovered that veering off the raked path meant getting stuck by sand burrs.

The only other place Emily could think of to look was the hotel restaurant. On her way there, she found him at the bank of public phones near the rest rooms.

At the sight of him, Emily felt a tingle race up her spine. Even though they were well and truly married, she still couldn't believe someone as brilliant and as handsome as Gabe wanted her in his life.

His back was to her as he cradled the receiver between his ear and shoulder while he took notes, but Emily would know the set of his shoulders anywhere—especially now that she'd explored every square inch of his body. She felt herself blush even though no one was around.

She decided to sneak up on him and cover his eyes from behind. It was a corny move, she knew, but she was in that kind of a mood. Honeymoons did that to a person.

"Yeah, I wish I could be there, too," he was saying as she crept up behind him. His sigh was filled with regret. "But you know how it is."

Emily stopped creeping.

"I've got a couple of offers I'm considering...you know, oil companies wanting to landscape around their drilling rigs and appease the environmentalists, that sort of thing."

He laughed, but it was a flat and unenthusiastic chuckle. It might fool the person he was talking to, but it didn't fool his new bride.

Something was bothering him. And if Gabe was bothered, then Emily was bothered.

"Not a desk job!" he protested. "No way. Not for any amount of money. I've got to have dirt under my fingernails." He checked his watch. "Hey, I forgot this was long distance. It'll probably cost me a fortune. Are you leaving Friday?" Gabe scrawled on what appeared to be one of the hotel's brochures. "Look, keep in touch. E-mail and maybe I can do some research from my end...they *don't?* You're kidding."

He slumped against the phone. "Well...I'll see you in a couple of years, I guess. Yeah. You, too." Slowly, he hung up the telephone and stared at it, lost in thought.

Emily's heart was beating so hard, she was surprised he couldn't hear it. "Gabe?"

He blinked at her an instant before recognition set in and he brightened. But Emily had seen his bleak expression before he'd composed it.

"Emily!" He winced and snapped his fingers. "You're waiting for your drink—I'm sorry." Gabe was smiling now...reaching for her hands...pulling her toward him, ready to kiss her. "Forgive me?"

Emily could fall into his arms and pretend that she'd seen and heard nothing, or...

Or she could turn her head so his kiss landed on her cheek. "Were you talking to Jason on the phone?" Jason had been his college roommate, and best man at their wedding.

It was a guess, but apparently a good one.

"Yeah." Gabe dropped her hands. "What do you say we go get those drinks?"

Say yes. She couldn't. "Jason's going on the Sahara project, isn't he?"

Gabe was in the process of draping an arm around her shoulders. He gave her a squeeze. "Yes. The team is leaving this weekend."

His arm slid away and he tugged on her hand. When she didn't walk forward he looked back.

Their gazes locked and held. A beat went by.

You want to go with them.

For Emily, it was one of those moments that sometimes happened in a person's life—a shuddering as though all the planets shook themselves into place. Looking into Gabe's eyes, everything became as crystal clear as the ocean she'd been snorkeling in every morning.

How could she have been so blind? "You wish you were going, too, don't you?"

Gabe looked away.

He can't meet my eyes.

"Well, sure. Hostile environment is my speciality," he said lightly.

"And nothing is more hostile than the Sahara Desert," she added, equally lightly.

He managed a smile. "It would have been a great opportunity, but it didn't work out."

"Why not?" she pressed, knowing his answer would change everything between them.

He must have known it, too, because instead of answering her, he dropped a light kiss on her lips. "Hey—don't worry about it." With his hand in the small of her back, he nudged her toward the bar. "There'll be other projects."

But not like this one. This is the chance of a lifetime.

It was as though Emily could hear the words Gabe didn't say.

Was that because she hadn't listened when he did say them? These last weeks, she'd been so involved with graduation and then coordinating the double wedding with Freddie that she and Gabe had hardly had an opportunity to be alone. Had she ignored something that was vitally important to him, or hadn't he mentioned it?

"If you wanted to go on the project, why didn't you say so?" she asked now. "We could have moved up the wedding." Although Freddie would have had a cow, but never mind. "In fact, we can still go on the Sahara project." Emily gripped his arm. "They aren't leaving until Friday, you said? That might be tight, but surely they wouldn't mind if we were a few days behind them."

The flicker of hope on his face made Emily plunge on, voicing plans as soon as she thought of them. "We can get the deposit back on the apartment. You haven't unpacked yet, and my stuff is still at Mom and Dad's. Or—I know. You go on ahead and I'll follow—''

"Emily," he interrupted her gently. "The Saudis won't allow women to work on the project."

"But *I* wouldn't be working."

"They don't want any foreign women entering the country. The area where they've built the Agro Center is on very remote Bedouin tribal land, and the government doesn't want to be responsible for the safety of females."

"But that's—''

"That's the way it is." He spoke with a flat finality.

So he'd given up going on a dream project in order to marry her. Emily's heart felt so full of love, she thought it might burst.

And then a chilling realization struck. *He'd given up going on a dream project in order to marry her.* Would he come to regret it? Did he already? "You still should have said something."

"What was there to say? It was go on the project or get married." He looped his arms around her waist and drew her close. "No contest."

His kiss failed to reassure her.

They'd reached the bar. "Your usual rum dinger with umbrella and extra fruit garnish?''

Emily nodded absently. She'd been so set on having a double wedding with Freddie, and since Hunter was going to law school, the wedding had to be in the summer before he started classes in the fall.

Did Gabe blame her?

With her new insight, Emily saw into the future—when they hit the inevitable rough patches in their marriage—of arguments beginning with, "Because of you, I couldn't go on the Sahara Project."

And even if he never mentioned it again, she'd always feel guilty.

This was no way to begin a marriage. He should have discussed it with her instead of making a major decision all by himself.

"I wish you'd told me."

"Emily, it's a nonissue. Forget it." He handed her the garish drink.

She took a big swallow. "I don't want to be the reason you aren't doing what you want to do. I want you to be happy. If figuring out how to grow crops in the Sahara means that much to you, then go."

"Emily, we waited all through school to get married. I didn't want to wait any longer."

She knew exactly how he felt, because she felt the same way. She'd thought the day of their wedding and the rest of their life together would never arrive. But... "You shouldn't have had to choose between marriage and an opportunity to work with Dr....Dr. Shelwhatshisname."

"Shelvinstein. Sometimes that's the way the pollen blows. Plant humor," he added wryly.

Oh, Gabe. "You could still go, and I think you should."

He stared at her. "For two years?"

Emily had been thinking of a few weeks. *I'll see you in a couple of years, I guess.* That's what he'd said to Jason. "Two ...*years?*"

Gabe nodded. "We need several generations of plants."

Emily heard the "we."

Gulping a sip of his drink, Gabe started explaining theory and practicality and cross fertilization and a dozen other reasons why the project would take a minimum of two years. Emily didn't pay attention to the scientific details. All she did was watch Gabe's face as it lit up with the fire of his enthusiasm. That passion for his work was one of the things she loved most about him.

She understood about wanting something that much—that's how she felt about having children.

Emily knew what she had to do: she had to give Gabe the chance to go on the project now, or he'd spend the rest of their marriage blaming her, whether or not he'd ever admit it. She'd already sensed the resentment, though he'd tried to conceal his feelings from her. She would prove to him that she could be mature and reasonable.

Emily stopped his torrent of words with a touch on his arm. "Gabe, if the project is that important to you—"

"Not just to me. This is global." He gestured with his hands. "We're talking about making a serious dent in world hunger. If this project is successful, it'll make a *huge* difference in people's lives."

"Then go."

"To the Sahara?"

"It's obvious that you've been thinking about the

project and wishing that you were going. I don't want to stand in your way.''

Admittedly, it was an empty gesture on Emily's part. In spite of all his rhetoric, once he thought about the logistics, she didn't believe he'd seriously consider leaving her for two years. Abandon her on their honeymoon? No. Not likely.

Emily waited for some variation of ''I love you too much to leave you now'' and then she saw his face, saw it transform with all the passion she wished would be directed at her—like the passion with which Hunter watched Freddie.

The passion she'd sensed was missing from her own marriage.

''You're sure?''

Her blood chilled at the sight of the hope in his eyes.

He plowed his fingers through his hair, bringing his hand to rest on the back of his neck. ''But, two years…what would you do while I was gone?''

He's seriously thinking about going. ''Law school,'' she managed through a mouth gone dry. She cleared her throat. ''This will give me the opportunity to go to law school.'' *Which I've never considered before this minute. Think! Have you ever heard me talk about law school? Freddie talked about law school. I never did. I just want to have babies.*

''Is that what you want to do?'' Gabe stared hard at her.

The question hung in the air. Emily couldn't

speak, so she forced herself to nod, one stiff bob of her head.

"It's perfect then," he said slowly.

Perfectly horrible.

"We'll both get to do what we want to do."

How am I supposed to have children when you're half-way around the world?

"I mean, you'll be in law school and you'd be studying all the time anyway...this could really work."

"You'd...you'd get to come home for visits?" Emily could hardly breathe, let alone speak.

"Of course!" Gabe hauled her to him in a fierce hug. "And we'll both be so busy, the time will go by fast."

Two years. Two years. Two years.

"I can't believe I can go after all." His voice started as an awed whisper, then became a shout of joy. "I can go!"

Emily fought back tears, but she needn't have bothered. Right then, Gabe wouldn't have noticed an approaching hurricane.

Stepping back from her, he stared at his watch. "The flight to Miami leaves at four. Maybe they've still got room on it!"

Grasping her shoulders, he drew her close once more and pressed his forehead to hers. "Emily, I have never loved you more than I do at this moment. I never dreamed..." He kissed her hard on the lips. "You're the best."

Emily felt nothing. She'd gone numb.

Gabe headed for the phones. "I *adore* you. When I get back, I'll make this up to you. I promise."

CHAPTER ONE

Ten years later

"YOU can give the baby back now, Emily. The mother has finished signing the consent form."

Emily Shaw looked up from the dark-haired cherub on her lap to the grinning, white-coated assistant at the EduPlaytion Toys consumer test lab.

"Hmm. I don't know," she said consideringly. "I'm thinking of keeping this one." She looked around at a room full of bright, primary-colored toys. "I'll bet I could find something to trade."

"Ask me again tonight after I've spent three hours pacing the floor with him." The baby's mother sighed. "He's teething."

"Poor little thing," Emily murmured sympathetically, though she'd never paced the floor with a teething baby.

A drop of drool spread across her yellow silk skirt.

"Oh…here." The mother rummaged in her diaper bag and thrust a burp cloth at Emily.

"It's okay. I won't melt." Emily truly didn't mind. There was nothing she'd mind about having a baby. Or lots of babies. She used the cloth to wipe his chin rather than dab at her skirt.

He blinked up at her with his huge brown eyes

before twisting in her lap and holding out his hands for his mother.

He looks just like Gabe—or Gabe's child. It was the eyes—that and the curly black hair and maybe the nose... Hastily, Emily held out the baby to his mother. Baby or not, anything that reminded her of her ex-husband after all this time was to be avoided.

"Is that everyone today?" she asked Nancy, the assistant.

"Yes, thank goodness." Nancy finished signing off on the form.

Wednesday was Early Childhood testing day. The days mothers could bring their children to play on the new toys had become so popular, that EduPlaytion had to make appointments now. As a company lawyer, one of Emily's jobs was to make sure that parents understood that these toys were prototypes and have them sign consent forms to that effect.

Though she maintained that she wanted to be available to answer questions, all the assistants knew Emily brought the consent forms down herself instead of sending her secretary because she wanted to look at the babies.

Nancy added the form to the others in her folder. "When are you going to stop coming down here and bouncing other women's babies on your knee and do something about having one of your own?"

Sooner than you think, Emily thought as she struggled off the child-sized green plastic chair. "When I find the right man."

"I hear you," Nancy said. "I swear, my daughter graduated two years ago and hasn't had a date since.

It's hard for a working woman to meet men. Too bad you can't order one from a catalog like you can everything else.''

Emily chuckled along with her though Nancy didn't know how close to the truth her words were.

The truth was, Emily had come to a momentous decision: She wanted a baby and she wanted one now. Well, at least she wanted to get started on having one now. She'd always wanted babies, so how had she reached the age of thirty-two without a baby in sight?

Because the thing about having babies was that a man had to be involved at some point, and Emily hadn't reached that point with any man since she'd divorced Gabriel Valera years ago.

She hadn't liked men a whole lot after Gabe and about the time she decided that they were part of the human race after all, her job as an intern in the district attorney's office hadn't allowed time for men. It had barely allowed time for her to pick up her dry cleaning.

So she'd quit and had gone to work as a corporate lawyer for a toy company. Toys and children went together, right? She saw kids every day and instead of cooling her baby fever, it raged unchecked.

No more.

"I'm taking off early this afternoon," she told Nancy. "So if there are any questions about the releases, direct them to Toby."

"Sure thing."

Two hours later, Emily pulled next to the curb in front of her friend Freddie's house, parked, took out her leather satchel and carefully closed the door on the first new car she'd bought since college.

It was a minivan with built-in child car seat, and the highest safety rating of any vehicle in its class.

Emily was aware that people were going to ask why a single attorney without a steady boyfriend had bought a minivan and had come up with several responses they might believe. In a few minutes, she'd try one out on Freddie.

In the meantime, she admired the van's palomino-gleam in the evening sun, beeped the alarm and headed up Freddie's pebbled front walk.

Freddie and Hunter lived in a perfect neighborhood for raising children—the fashionable West University area in Houston. Close to the Galleria's shopping and equally close to the museums, it avoided the sterile, fast-food chained sameness of suburbia.

It was also very pricey, but several years of dual attorney incomes had taken care of that.

According to their grand plan, she and Freddie were supposed to buy houses next to each other. Freddie seemed to have forgotten that, though Emily couldn't have afforded anything in this neighborhood, anyway. However, it had the big yards and tall trees just like they'd imagined their homes would have.

Suburbia wasn't so bad. Emily had been living in her three bedroom, two bath house out west and commuting for three months now. She had not one, but two trees, and though they wouldn't support a swing for several years, they would someday. And with the purchase of the minivan, she was all set for motherhood.

She patted her leather satchel. Well, almost.

As she approached the giant terra-cotta urns near the entryway, the red front door opened and a harried Freddie waved her inside.

"Wait a minute—did you drive up in that?" She pointed over Emily's shoulder.

"Yes," Emily began and readied the favorite of her explanations. She never got to use it.

"Your car is in the shop *again?* Didn't they have anything for you to rent but that? I keep telling you to buy a new one."

"Actually—"

"Come in, you're letting all the air conditioning out." Freddie pulled her across the threshold. "Hunter grumbled about our *outrageous* bill last month. And you know how he can be."

Emily had never thought of the elegant Hunter as *grumbling.*

Freddie was on the move, her mules clicking across the imported Italian tile—one of about a hundred patterns she'd shown Emily when Emily had suffered through the redecorating saga with her. "The breakfast room is officially party central," Freddie called back over her shoulder. "I've got samples of decorations spread all over and they're all so cute, I can't decide which theme to use. You're such a doll to help me with this."

Emily followed her through the cavernous dining room, where she'd been the unattached female at dozens of Freddie's corporate dinners, and into the kitchen. "This place does look festive." She lifted garish green, orange and yellow decorations off one of the chairs. "I think we can eliminate this set."

Freddie laughed and ran her fingers distractedly through her short brown hair, then had to reclip the barrette. Ends stuck out every which way making her look like the nine-year-old Fredericka-and-don't-you-dare-call-me-anything-but-Freddie she'd been when Emily had moved into their old neighborhood. "My secretary said I needed to loosen up."

"Not this loose." Emily also rejected a cloyingly sweet pastel rose theme and was thinking real hard about the sunflowers. Freddie wasn't a flower person.

Emily was, not that it mattered to anyone.

"Well...she also told me people are starting to call me 'ice princess.'"

"And this bothers you?"

"Well, yeah! It's 'ice queen' or nothing!"

They both laughed.

"What do the invitations look like?" Emily was actually here to address the invitations to Hunter and Freddie's anniversary party. She was mentally avoiding the fact that it was also *her* anniversary.

"They look like invitations." Freddie picked up the top box of a three-box stack and opened it to reveal two rows of cards and envelopes.

Just how many people did she plan to invite?

Freddie held up a cream panel with dark gray engraving. It might have been an announcement that a new law office was opening.

"I see what you mean," Emily said. "I guess it's a formal party then."

Freddie flipped the rectangle around and stared at it, then looked at Emily, her dimples barely held in check.

Emily had seen that expression countless times in the past, so she waited, and sure enough Freddie's face creased into a full-fledged grin. "Oh, Em, I can't stand it! Yes, I want a party to end all parties because...because it is, I guess."

This sounded intriguing. Emily slipped her satchel strap off her shoulder and slid onto the chair. "Okay, talk."

"It's time," Freddie announced dramatically, then dumped an angel theme set on the floor and sat in the chair across from Emily.

"Time for what?" Emily responded to her cue.

"To have a baby."

Since this was the way Emily had been thinking for months, she didn't realize immediately that Freddie had echoed her strongest desire.

"You look so stunned," Freddie said. "For goodness' sake, Hunter and I've been married ten years. You're the *only* person who hasn't stared at my waist the morning after I've gorged myself on a huge Mexican food meal and hinted that they expected a forthcoming announcement."

Actually, Emily *had* been watching Freddie's waist—she just hadn't mentioned anything. "You always said you wanted a career," she commented lamely.

"And I have one. Here, let's toast—oh! I forgot the drinks!"

Her laugh noticeably shrill, Freddie flew to the

refrigerator and withdrew two tall glasses and a plastic container.

What was with her, anyway? She sounded like a woman on the edge.

Emily couldn't see what she was doing at the counter until Freddie turned around.

"Ta da!" The drinks she held out were decorated with fruit garnishes and paper umbrellas.

One of the drinks had two sticks of fruit.

Emily felt like she'd been sandbagged. Emotions in turmoil, she was instantly transported to the scene of her broken honeymoon. Even after all this time, the smell of rum and pineapple juice made her nauseous. Her wounds felt as fresh as though they'd been inflicted yesterday. She could clearly see Gabe's face as he waved and blew her two-handed kisses from the tiny prop plane that would fly him off the island and out of her life. Considering that her eyes had been full of tears at the time, Emily was surprised she had such a clear mental image.

Heartbreak had obviously sharpened it.

But she'd never revealed anything to an incredulous Freddie, even after hours of relentless questions, and she wasn't going to now.

Emily forced herself to take the drink. As her fingers closed around the tumbler, she felt the cold seep from her fingers down her arm and straight into her heart.

An oblivious Freddie chinked her glass against Emily's. "I have no idea what's in a rum dinger besides rum, but I had a whole lot of fun trying different things. Here's to the success of the last ten years."

Emily couldn't will herself to drink Freddie's concoction. Her mouth was dry. Her fingers wouldn't work. Her arm wouldn't bend. What was the matter with her? Ten years had gone by. Ten. She was so over Gabriel Valera.

"Emily?"

Emily swallowed.

"Oh gosh." Freddie snatched the drink out of Emily's hand, hurried over to the sink and threw the contents of both glasses down the drain. Then she ran water and turned on the disposal, grinding up the bamboo skewers and paper umbrellas as well as the fruit and ice.

The room was suddenly quiet. "I'm sorry Emily—I didn't think. And to ask you to help me with the invitations to my anniversary party—when it's also *your* anniversary…" She covered her mouth with her fingers. "I've been so selfishly insensitive."

"As you say, it's been ten years." Emily was finally able to speak. "I'm…I'm surprised it's bothering me. It shouldn't. Maybe it was because I saw this baby today and he looked like Gabe and I've…" Her throat tightened before she could add, "been thinking about having a baby, too."

"Let's just forget the invitations and have dinner." Freddie jerked open the refrigerator door. "Lupe made that Chinese chicken salad you like."

Emily swallowed again. It was easier now. "I am looking forward to the salad, but I can still help you address invitations."

Freddie hesitated in front of the refrigerator.

"No." She pulled out a large bowl. "Hunter should be the one helping me anyway."

Hunter hated Chinese chicken salad, so that told Emily that he wasn't coming home in time for dinner. For a busy attorney, that was hardly unusual. "Is he working on a case?"

"He's always working on a case." Freddie set the bowl down with a thud.

Oops. Time for a change of subject. "So I'll address invitations. I don't mind, truly. And I'd hate to think I wasted a trip over here—not that seeing you isn't reason enough to brave the freeways."

Freddie gave her a look. "Why *did* you buy a house way out in the boondocks, anyway?"

Here was her opportunity to tell Freddie about her baby plans. Ideally, Freddie should be the first to know, even before Emily's mother. In fact, her mother probably shouldn't be told until the actual birth.

Freddie was her best friend. Her reaction would give Emily a taste of what she could expect from other people.

She tucked her hair behind both ears, then dropped her hands. She'd been told—by Freddie—that she put her hair behind her ears right before she said something she felt was iffy. It was a "tell" and something to avoid in the courtroom. Emily didn't practice in the courtroom anymore, but Freddie did.

"Emily!" she pounced immediately. "What's going on? Have you met someone? Are you—you didn't elope and not tell me, did you?" She dropped silverware on the table and grabbed Emily's hand to look for a ring.

"Of course not." Emily pulled her hand away. "I'm going to have a baby."

Freddie plopped onto the chair with all the grace of a water buffalo. "How—when... *who?*"

That "who" pretty much said it all. Obviously Emily would never be able to consider a career as a woman of mystery. "Not for a while, of course."

"I can *see* that." Freddie gestured toward Emily's waist.

"I'm not pregnant! Well, not yet."

"You sure know how to scare a person." Freddie propped her head on her fist. "I wish I had that drink back."

"Want me to pour you some wine?"

Freddie shook her head. "I have a feeling I'm going to want to concentrate." She sat up straight and fixed Emily with her lawyer look. "Start at the beginning."

"Aren't you going to take notes?"

"Should I?"

Emily sighed. "I want kids. I've always wanted kids."

"And we planned to have them after we established ourselves."

"*You* decided. I never wanted to wait."

Freddie blinked. If she hadn't still been wearing her professional face, Emily imagined she'd have been able to see the struggle not to ask Emily about Gabe.

Then again, maybe she was exaggerating the impact of a five-day marriage.

"If you felt that way, why did you never remarry?"

"Maybe you don't realize how hard it is for a working girl to meet men," she answered, borrowing from the earlier conversation with Nancy.

"I've introduced you to a ton of men! Dinner after dinner after dinner, I've sat you next to some real cuties and waited for the sparks to flash."

And all this time, Emily had thought she was doing Freddie a favor by coming. "Those were business dinners! You didn't want me flirting with your colleagues and clients."

"Of course I did!"

"I went out with a couple," Emily said defensively.

"After I practically forced you. Look, I never pressed you to tell me what happened between you and Gabe—"

"Oh, yes you did!"

"Not after you convinced me that you didn't want to talk about it." She looked directly at Emily. "You're my best friend and all this time I've had to wonder why he left for that project and never came back."

Regrettably true. "He left because I told him to."

"Why?"

"Because I didn't think he would."

Freddie did deserve more of an explanation, so Emily reiterated her reasoning at the time.

Freddie rolled her eyes when Emily finished. "You realize that if you'd told me this back then, I would have knocked both your heads together and you'd still be married?"

"But he would have resented me!"

"So I would have knocked his head extra hard."

Freddie stood and silently set the table. It wasn't until she'd served two glasses of iced tea and the bowl of salad that she spoke again. ''Don't think you've succeeded in making me forget the baby remark. What are you planning?''

''Artificial insemination.''

''Thought it all through?'' Freddie asked calmly.

''Yes,'' Emily replied with equal calm. She reached for her satchel. ''I've brought some information with me and I also printed some donor catalog entries from the Internet.''

''You mean you can order your baby's father off the *Internet?*'' Freddie reached for the catalog pages Emily had printed out.

''That's kind of for do-it-yourselfers.''

''You don't expect *me*—''

''Of course not! I doubt that I'll use these particular banks,'' Emily reassured her. ''But I was interested in reading the profiles so I'll know what to expect when I go to whichever bank my doctor recommends.''

''I can't believe this. I tell you, Emily, the world is just getting weirder and weirder. It makes you think twice before bringing a child into it.''

''I've already thought twice. More than twice. I've been planning this for a year.'' It was important that Freddie understand that this wasn't some whim of Emily's.

''I know, I know.'' Freddie squeezed extra lemon into her iced tea. ''Don't worry, I'm not changing my mind, but it *is* a serious step.''

Emily exhaled. ''Good. I have to tell you, know-

ing that you'll be having a baby at the same time
means the world to me."

"It's what we always planned."

"I know, but, well, we didn't plan on me being
a single mother..." She swallowed. "But at least
when our kids are playing together at your house,
my baby can be around Hunter. He'll be a great
father, Freddie."

When Freddie looked down and squeezed a third
lemon wedge into her tea, Emily knew something
was wrong. "How does he feel about 'project pregnancy'?"

Freddie ripped open a packet of sweetener. She
never sweetened her tea. "I haven't told him."

"When *are* you going to tell him you want to get
pregnant?"

"Our anniversary."

"That'll be a good present." Emily sighed,
briefly indulging in a fit of what-ifs.

"I hope so!" Freddie held up crossed fingers.
"But, hey, let's check out these profiles you've
marked. I have final approval, you know."

"You do not!"

"We're talking about the father of my future
child's best friend, here. How many mothers can
have that much influence on their kids' friends?"

Emily spread out the catalog forms. "You know
something? I'd hate to have you for a mother-in-
law."

Freddie grabbed her hand. "Oh, Emily! Wouldn't
that just be—" She squeezed Emily's hand before
releasing it. "These are more important than ever."
She picked up one of the sheets. "We might be de-

ciding the genetic makeup of my grandchildren.''
She pointed to a number Emily had highlighted. ''A
bodybuilder? I don't want my future grandchild having a bodybuilder for a grandfather.''

Emily struggled not to laugh. ''What have you
got against bodybuilders?''

''Aren't there any attorneys listed?''

''Haven't you got enough lawyers in the family?''

''Never. Daddy is counting on me to grow him a
dynasty.'' Freddie, whose full name was Fredericka
Welles Loren Cole, though she didn't use Hunter's
last name professionally, worked with her father—
Frederick Welles Loren—in his law firm. Hunter
had chosen to practice elsewhere.

It made for some tense conversations at those dinners they were always inviting Emily to. She was
glad she was with a toy firm. Toys didn't argue unless they were supposed to.

Freddie scanned the sheets, then quietly tamped
them together before looking directly at Emily.

''What?''

''Other than the bodybuilder, every candidate you
marked is either a doctor or a chemist or other sci-
entist of some sort.''

''So?''

''Listen to these—brown hair, brown eyes, five-
eleven, chemist. Brown hair, brown eyes, six-two,
medical student. Brown hair, brown eyes, six-even,
biology teacher. And then this one—*naturally curly*
brown hair, brown eyes, six-one, an economist.''
She looked at Emily, then continued, ''And when
we read the expanded profile of this one we find that
Donor 1143 enjoys studying the natural sciences and

hopes to train others to employ better farming meth-ods. Sound like anybody we know?''

Emily pretended to be engrossed in picking out the chicken in her salad.

"Emily, they're all Gabe clones!"

Gabe, Gabe, Gabe. Why was it that after all these Gabe-free years he was turning up in nearly every other conversation and thought? "Brown hair and brown eyes is common. *I* have brown hair and brown eyes. And why wouldn't I want an intelligent father for my child?"

Freddie scanned the donor profiles for about a nanosecond before reading off two blond-haired, blue-eyed medical students.

"There must have been something I didn't like in their expanded profiles," Emily said casually. "A family history of heart disease, maybe. I don't know why you keep bringing Gabe up."

Freddie gave her a long look, then shrugged with elaborate unconcern. "All right, fine. I won't mention him again." She picked at her salad, then asked, "So after you choose one of these...these daddy candidates, then what?"

Emily told Freddie everything she'd discovered about the procedure. "What do you think?"

Freddie made a face. "Emily, it's so...I think you ought to hold off until you meet this great guy in our office who'd be just perfect for you. Granted, he's a couple of years younger, but that shouldn't bother—"

"Freddie. I've made up my mind. And I don't want only one baby—I want several. I'm already getting a late start."

"You're not just saying this because Hunter and I are ready to try for a family? I know what we always said about our kids growing up together, but we were just kids ourselves."

"Haven't you been listening? I've been thinking about this for a long time. I've made plans. I'm ready."

Freddie was silent. Emily knew she was thinking, and experience had taught her it was best just to let her think. But while she was thinking, Emily realized how important Freddie's support was to her and the longer Freddie was silent, the more nervous Emily became.

"You're sure?" Freddie asked at last.

"Yes."

A slow grin stole across Freddie's face. "I'm so *glad* I won't have to get fat by myself!"

CHAPTER TWO

"TELL me about Emily Shaw."

Great. Just when he thought he'd breezed through the multi-week screening sessions with this doctor the way he had all the others, she had to bring up Emily.

Gabe shifted in the leather wing chair. The darn thing was supposed to be comfortable, he supposed, but it wasn't. He kept slipping down in the tightly-stuffed seat.

Or maybe the chair wasn't supposed to be comfortable at all so Dr. Melinda Weber's patients would choose to lie on the couch the way psychiatric patients did in movies.

No thanks. They were both sitting on the same side of her desk and that's the way he wanted it. He was no psychiatric patient, or at least not the usual one. He was here because he had to be. Dr. Weber was evaluating him the way she was evaluating everyone who was scheduled to spend the next two years sealed away in a biosphere under controlled conditions. Strictly routine. He'd had these screenings before and would again.

Except she was the first doctor to ask him about Emily. Also the first woman doctor he'd had. There was probably a connection.

"Does the thought of discussing Emily Shaw make you uncomfortable?"

"What?" He shifted again, then forced himself to sit still. After a mental check of his body language to make sure it remained open, confident, and re-laxed—he could play this game, too—Gabe contin-ued with studied casualness. "Oh, Emily. No, talk-ing about her doesn't bother me, but that was a long time ago and I was surprised to hear you ask. We were in love—or I was. Technically, we got married, but it didn't last. End of story."

He shouldn't have said "technically."

Sure enough, Dr. Weber made a note. Gabe hated it when she did that. Next time, he'd request a male psychiatrist, except then they'd probably think he had issues with women.

Whatever. This was all a waste of time. Dr. Weber wasn't going to find any reason to prohibit him from going into the biosphere. He was in charge of the project, for one thing, and for another, he was the best in his field. He'd tell her, if she gave him the chance. It wasn't boasting, and it was a fact more important than the details of a first love gone sour.

"You say you were 'technically' married. Does that mean you received an annulment?"

Images from his long-ago honeymoon surfed through his mind. "No. We divorced."

"How long did your marriage last?"

Gabe's leg muscle tensed, but he stopped himself from moving just in time. How to answer?

"Can't you remember?"

He remembered. He remembered everything.

"We were married. Big blowout. It was a double wedding, in fact."

That got her pencil moving.

"The wedding was scheduled right before the beginning of the Sahara Project." Which obviously meant nothing to her. Struggling to keep the impatience out of his voice, he explained, "It was a major project involving developing crops that would grow in hostile environments—specifically arid conditions. My speciality."

She didn't bother noting it, he saw.

"Fully-funded opportunities like that don't come along often, especially for brand-new graduates." He waited and still she wrote nothing. And these were the important facts.

Doggedly, Gabe continued, "Because of the wedding, I didn't go and Emily found out about it while we were on our honeymoon. She told me I should go." He leaned forward. "*Insisted* I go. So I did."

"When?"

"A few hours later."

Dr. Weber blinked. "You left her on your *honeymoon?*" she asked with unprofessional incredulity.

Gabe raised his eyebrow.

She didn't back down. "How long were you gone?"

"The project was originally scheduled to last two years. Emily knew that, by the way." He didn't appreciate looking like the bad guy in the situation.

"Since this was such a long-term project, I assume she went with you?"

Gabe shook his head. "It was in Saudi Arabia. She wasn't allowed."

"Did she know that as well?"

It was veiled, but he heard the sarcasm. "Yes."

More scribbling. Lots of scribbling. Too much scribbling. In the middle of it all, Dr. Weber tucked her hair behind her ear just the way Emily used to.

The two women were nothing alike. Nothing. Sure, they both had brown hair, but it had been a long time since women with chin-length brown hair automatically reminded him of Emily. Her hair had brushed her shoulders the last time he'd seen her. He liked it longer.

"How did you feel when she told you to go?"

"Overjoyed," he replied honestly. "This was my dream. Not only that, but I'd get about ten years experience in two years." Gabe shifted before he caught himself. Oh, what the heck. "Emily wanted to go to law school. This way, she could go full-time and concentrate on her studies rather than drawing it out for years as a part-time student. It seemed perfect."

"So what happened?"

"I don't know." And he didn't, but it was obviously the wrong thing to say, which he would have realized if he'd been on his guard. "At some point, she evidently changed her mind."

"Did you discuss it?"

"I wasn't given the opportunity."

Melinda Weber looked as if she wanted to comment but made one of her irritating notes, instead. "Did she go to law school?"

"Yes."

"And were you away for two years?"

"Yes." Then, figuring he was already in too deep, Gabe added, "Actually, I stayed on an extra year. But Emily had another year of law school, too, along with internships where she ended up working twelve- to fourteen-hour days. I wouldn't have seen much of her anyway."

Dr. Weber looked at him. "How often did you see each other during that time?"

Might as well tell her everything. Maybe she'll be able to tell me what went wrong. I sure as hell don't know. "I came back to the States after the two years and told Emily that the project was funded for a third year."

"Was that the first time you two had seen each other since you left?"

Gabe nodded, conscious of how bad it sounded to an outsider. Even though Emily had law school expenses and his stipend was barely enough to cover his living expenses—let alone save for airfare home—he'd never thought two years would pass before he and Emily saw each other again. Fate had other plans. "The Gulf War," he reminded the doctor.

An expression he thought might have been sympathy crossed her face.

"When I came back, I would have stayed, but since Emily was still in school, she agreed with me going back for another year. I thought we were going to be set up for the good life. I already had job offers—I could have gone anywhere she wanted to practice law. Then a few weeks later, she served me with divorce papers. That seemed to be what she wanted, so I signed them.''

''*Seemed* to be? Don't you know?''

No, he didn't know. He'd missed Emily like crazy. He'd thought she'd missed him, too. The divorce papers had stunned him. After reading them over and over, he'd immediately commandeered one of the project Hummers and had driven off into the desert. He hadn't gotten very far, which was a good thing because he hadn't taken any water or supplies—or his passport—and had only the vaguest idea of where the nearest city was.

Days later, on one of the official supply trips into town, he'd spent the entire time futilely trying to place an international call. He'd repeated the exercise every trip for a month, trading all his free days for the next quarter before he'd had to give up.

''If she hadn't wanted me to go back for the third year, why didn't she say something?'' he asked Dr. Weber now. ''It took weeks to get letters back and forth and they were always censored. What was I supposed to do? I figured she'd met somebody else and hadn't wanted to tell me in person.''

He may have been imagining it, but Dr. Weber seemed to have thawed a little. ''And had she?''

''I don't know. She wasn't married when I came back.''

''Do you keep in touch?''

Gabe shook his head. ''We, ah, met for lunch and it…'' Had been a disaster. ''There wasn't anything to talk about.''

The Emily who'd met him for lunch that day was nothing like the Emily he'd married, or the Emily he'd gone to school with. Not nearly as soft or as wide-eyed. But lawyers weren't. Still, he'd thought that maybe they could start over again—definitely without her friend Freddie calling all the shots.

They'd ordered drinks and she'd acted as cold as the ice in the glasses. He was already wondering how he could endure the lunch when his pager had gone off. It was only the low-battery warning, but he'd used the excuse to escape the awkward atmosphere.

The doctor was writing in earnest now, but Gabe didn't care. "You're a woman, what do you think happened?"

"My gender is not relevant."

"Sure it is. None of the other docs ever asked about Emily."

"I can't speculate," she said, "but anyone would realize that a long separation strains a relationship. You two barely had one to sustain."

"Sure we did. We dated all through college." Gabe smiled faintly. "I was a year ahead of her— we met when I was her lab assistant in botany during her freshman year. I never went out with anyone else after I met her."

"And you never remarried."

"No, but don't think I'm carrying a torch for her. I'm not married because I haven't met anyone else I wanted to marry. I don't have anything against marriage. Or women," he added just to cover all the bases.

That prompted a smile. "I wasn't implying that you did. However you asked me to speculate about what happened to your relationship with Emily. Without talking with her, I can't know for sure. And neither can you. Therefore…"

Gabe didn't like the sound of that "therefore."

"I am recommending that you meet with her and ask her the questions you obviously need answered."

"I don't *need* them answered." That was the past. They'd both moved on.

"I believe you do. According to your test results, you have difficulty with verbal subtexts and interpersonal judgments."

What kind of mumbo jumbo was that? "If people say what they mean, then we get along fine."

Dr. Weber sat back and placed her notes on her desk. "I'm charged with evaluating the personalities which will be living together on this project. I have concerns—"

"Oh, come on." Gabe couldn't believe what he was hearing. "That was ten years ago. I was just a green kid."

He might not have spoken.

"I have concerns about your ability to formulate effective methods of diffusing interpersonal conflicts."

"You mind speaking English?"

She took off her glasses. "You've never been in a long-term relationship and have lived alone since your brief marriage. That failed, and you have no idea why. Find out, or I won't approve you for the biosphere project.''

That was blunt. He could be equally blunt. Gabe stood. He could handle either the chair or the doctor, but not both at the same time. "I was twenty-three. That's what happened. Believe me, I'm older, wiser and busier." He smiled the smile that had convinced many a hesitant sponsor to donate money. "Aren't you?"

She didn't smile back.

Okay, so he *couldn't* handle the doctor. But he wasn't going to sit in her damn chair anymore, either.

"Mr. Valera, I have to assess not only your personality and how it meshes with your potential team, but your ability to do the same thing once you're on your own with them."

He knew where she was going with this. "It's been my experience that if people are busy, they don't have time to get on each other's nerves."

"I don't believe you're taking this seriously."

He'd had enough. "I'm very serious. These people are going to have a job to do. It's their number one priority and they should be left alone and allowed to do it. If they've got personality problems, then it's *your* job to find that out before they ever make it inside the biosphere. Find me a good team, Dr. Weber. That's all I ask."

"You're also asking me to ignore my professional concerns about you."

"Because I made a mistake and got married when I shouldn't have?"

She leveled a very doctorly look at him. "Because you don't understand why your marriage failed."

"That has nothing to do with this."

"Yes, it does." She ticked off reasons on her fingers. "You two had a contract. You were starting a 'project.' You invested money. You were going to live together somewhere new. Something went wrong. The only difference is that you never had to write a final report analysis. I'm asking you to do so now."

Gabe stared at her. She was making sense. He hated it when that happened. "You're good."

"Thanks."

They eyed each other a moment longer, then Gabe grabbed the doorknob. "Okay. I'll find Emily and we'll hash this out. You find me a good team."

Emily was engrossed in a distribution contract for the latest educational video game, one in which math warriors sliced numbers into fractions. Why did arithmetic have to be so violent? she wondered as the message light flashed on her phone.

She ignored it. Toby, her assistant, was screening her calls until Emily finished going over the contract, which had to be completed by lunch. Some days, it seemed the phone never stopped ringing. Today was one of those days.

Moments after the light stopped blinking, Toby tapped on the door and stuck her head in.

Emily frowned at her, but Toby came in anyway. Quickly gliding across the carpet, she put a pink message slip on Emily's desk, then pivoted and made her escape.

Wondering what crisis was developing now, Emily reached for the paper.

Gabriel Valera.

Her breath caught as she stared at the name written in Toby's loopy handwriting.

This must be Freddie's idea of a joke.

"Toby!" she called, not bothering with the intercom.

"He *told* me you'd want to know," Toby's voice came from the other side of the closed door.

He?

"Toby—" Emily broke off and punched the intercom button on her phone system. "Toby—"

The door opened. Emily looked up at her assistant. "I'm on the intercom now. You didn't have to get up from your desk."

"I wasn't at my desk. I was listening at your door in case you called this guy back."

"You admit to eavesdropping? That's not the way it works."

"I'm hoping you'll be so impressed by my honesty, you'll tell me who that guy is."

Emily smiled reluctantly. "So a man left this message—it wasn't Freddie Loren?"

Toby shook her head. "He's called three times, too."

Gabe, himself, had actually called her. Three times.

"Thanks, Toby," she said, ignoring her assistant's disappointed expression.

Gabe had called. *Three times.* Emily punched through the messages in her electronic mailbox. He'd called yesterday, but she'd already left to see Freddie. Twice again this morning. Hesitantly, she played one of the messages and Gabe's rich baritone was saying his name and telephone number. "Say, Em," he continued with an easy familiarity undiminished by time, "when you've got a few minutes, I'd like to talk with you. Give me a call."

Talk with her about what? Why was he calling her? Why now after all these years? Why now, when she was planning for a baby?

More important—should she return his call? That would be the logical thing to do, but what if he wanted to see her? At the thought, she felt queasy. She'd met Gabe for lunch that one time about a year after their divorce, and had been proud of the way she'd handled herself. Then the drinks had barely arrived before he'd rushed off for some work crisis that required his immediate attention. And just what possible emergency could plants have? Dehydration? Chlorophyll allergies?

No. She'd been right to break off with him and go on with her life.

Emily glanced at the phone number next to his name, then crumpled the pink paper and threw it into the wastebasket. She didn't want to see or speak to Gabe Valera ever again. She didn't have to. And she wouldn't.

Irritated, Gabe punched off his cell phone and went back to cataloging seedlings. Emily still hadn't returned any of his calls. Gabe wasn't quite to the point where he knew for certain Emily was avoiding him, but it was close.

He'd been surprised to discover that she'd moved and he didn't have her new telephone number. It had bothered him that he didn't know where she was living. Even though he hadn't spoken to or seen her in years, Gabe had always known where Emily was. Why, he couldn't say. Maybe in the back of his mind, he'd hoped that when her anger had cooled, they could start over.

But the time had never seemed right.

Fortunately, she still worked at EduPlaytion, so he'd been calling her there, for all the good it had done him.

"Hey, Gabe."

Gabe didn't bother looking up from his plants. "You have that tone in your voice again, Larry. The tone that tells me you're going to bother me with petty administrative details."

"Give me a break, Gabe."

"I pay you a fortune so I won't have to be bothered with petty administrative details."

"You pay me to know the difference between petty and interesting."

He did. Reluctantly, Gabe scribbled a few notes so he could take up where he'd left off and set his clipboard on the wooden ledge underneath the seedling shelves. "What's up?"

Dressed in a suit and tie, Larry Ciner, president of Nutritional Engineering, stood before him sweating in the arid conditions of the lab's greenhouse. "Publicity."

Gabe groaned.

"You don't know what I'm going to say yet."

"I can guess."

"Toys."

"I wouldn't have guessed that," Gabe admitted.

Larry didn't smile. Gabe wished he had more of a sense of humor.

"The NASA publicity department wants a biosphere toy tie-in to keep the public's interest in the project. Next year is an election year and we don't want funds drying up when a new congress starts hacking at the budget."

"Sounds good." Gabe reached for his clipboard.

"You have to give a press conference."

He hated this part of his job. He was good at it, but he hated it. "When and where?"

"Thursday, downtown, at the Texas Plaza Hotel."

Over the years, Gabe had trained Larry into giving him only the bare facts. Sometimes Larry took this to extremes. "The usual dog and pony show?"

"Yeah." Larry, face flushed, edged down the gravel aisle toward the door.

"Remind me tomorrow, okay?"

"Sure thing."

As Larry's footsteps crunched on the gravel, Gabe reached for his clipboard when an idea came to him. "Larry!"

He paused and slowly turned back, his expression beleaguered.

"EduPlaytion."

Larry nodded. "Good company. They'll certainly be invited to bid on the toy tie-in."

"No bids."

Larry's eyes widened. "But—"

Gabe held up a hand and stopped his protest. "Offer them the contract—contingent on Emily Shaw handling the legalities. Tell them it's a deal breaker."

"Emily, have you got a minute?"

Since the question was being asked by Bill Stone, one of the vice presidents of EduPlaytion, Emily knew it was a rhetorical question.

"Sure." Smoothing her skirt, and momentarily wishing she were dressed in important navy blue and not green, Emily stepped from behind her desk and gestured toward the club chairs in front of it.

The vice president had come to her and not called her to him. Whatever the reason, it was bound to be interesting.

"I've had a request," he began as they sat. "NASA and a company called Nutritional Engineering are involved in a joint biosphere project to develop strains of plants that can survive and produce food under harsh climate conditions."

He paused and Emily understood that he expected some reaction from her. Since she'd never heard of this project, there wasn't anything she could react to, but it sounded like a Gabe project if ever there was one.

But she'd promised herself not to think about Gabe. "Yes?" she said noncommittally.

"We've been offered a contract to develop a line of scientific toys to go along with it." He paused again, his gaze sweeping over her, then went on. "It would be the largest toy contract in the history of EduPlaytion."

Emily was dying to know what all this had to do with her. She was not a senior level lawyer, by any means.

"Naturally, this interests us."

"Naturally."

"Emily," he said, his tone completely different. "Do you know anyone at NASA or Nutritional Engineering?"

She shook her head. "Why?"

"Because they want you as the legal representative."

"Me? Are you sure?" she blurted out before realizing how questioning the vice president would sound.

"Very sure" was his dry response. "We've been made to understand that your participation is not a negotiable point."

Emily just stared at him.

"Under other circumstances, I would prefer that you had a little more seasoning, but I believe that you're capable of handling the contract details of a deal this large. I want you to know that you will have access to all the resources of our legal department and any additional clerical personnel you'll need. This also means we'll have to redistribute your current projects.''

Emily found her voice. "I don't understand...this isn't even my field!"

He leveled a look at her. "Now it is." He stood preparing to leave, so Emily did as well. "I'll want to be kept apprised of all developments. Daily if necessary.''

"Of course.''

He nodded. "I'll tell them to proceed then and have my assistant prepare you a brief.''

"Bill?"

Halfway to the door, he stopped and turned.

Emily tilted up her chin, but her palms were moist. "If I'm going to be in charge of the largest contract in the history of EduPlaytion, then I want a title and a salary that reflects that.''

Surprise and something Emily decided was relieved admiration flitted across his face. "You'll do, Emily.''

He nodded and was smiling as he left the room.

Thoughtfully, Emily gazed after him, a dark suspicion creeping through her.

CHAPTER THREE

FOUR hours. They'd given her a measly *four* hours notice before her first big meeting. There was a press conference that Emily had no hope of making, then a joint meeting with representatives of NASA and Nutritional Engineering.

The promised brief wasn't even finished. She'd barely had time for a hurried conference with the head of EduPlaytion's design team, who'd be late in joining her at the meeting. Fortunately, she was familiar with tie-in contracts and knew better than to guarantee any details until she'd had an opportunity to study the situation, but Emily was angry.

She'd been offered the chance of a lifetime, one that had made Freddie hugely impressed and even a little jealous. Freddie had *never* been jealous of Emily.

Emily hadn't even had a chance to savor the sensation when all this had been dumped on her.

She suspected she was being set up to fail and didn't like it. No one could have been prepared in such a short time. Send her in ill-prepared and inexperienced, would they? If the people responsible for requesting her on this deal thought they'd capitalize on her inexperience, they were wrong. She wouldn't be pushed into anything.

Emily drew a deep breath. All these vows to herself were great when she was in her office, but now she was getting off the elevator and heading to a conference room at the venerable Texas Plaza Hotel, specifically, the Longhorn room, adorned with mounted steer horns and decorated in leathers and framed branding irons.

Very Texan. Very male. She wouldn't be surprised to open the door to the aroma of cigars and whiskey.

Emily had chosen to wear a summer-weight black-and-white suit that made her appear important without looking like she was trying to appear important. Feminine, yet competent. Texan men expected their truly powerful women to retain a touch of femininity.

She pushed open the massive wooden doors and scanned the knot of men standing over by the windows, looking for a familiar face.

Looking, she realized, for Gabe.

She looked like a million bucks.

Gabe had come straight from the press conference, hoping that Emily would be early so their first meeting in years wouldn't take place so publicly.

If she'd bothered to return his calls, then it wouldn't have.

She hadn't seen him yet. He didn't know if she *expected* to see him. Or if she'd care.

An unfamiliar feeling invaded the pit of his stomach—a feeling he identified with surprise as nerves. He was actually nervous about seeing Emily again.

At this point in their lives she should be nothing

more than an old friend. A very good old friend. Or maybe an angry old friend.

Or maybe not a friend at all, he realized as her gaze swept the room.

"Gabe?" One of the NASA publicity hotshots he'd been talking to looked over his shoulder. "Well...who do we have here?" he asked with a definite male interest.

The other men Gabe had been talking to turned as one. As their appreciative murmurs rumbled quietly, another unfamiliar emotion surged through Gabe—possessiveness. He suddenly realized he didn't want these young wolves drooling over Emily.

If anybody was going to drool over Emily, then it was going to be— "That would be Emily Shaw, the EduPlaytion attorney," he said before he had a chance to complete his thought.

Knowing he had no right to these feelings didn't stop Gabe from breaking away from the group to approach her and let these young men on the prowl know they'd have to get by him first.

The glare from the panoramic windows kept the men's faces in shadow, but Emily could sense them staring at her. Fine. Let them stare.

She walked over to the oval conference table and set her briefcase on it. Flipping open the lock, she reached for the regrettably slim file she had on the project.

One of the men broke away from the others. "Emily."

It had been years since she'd heard that familiar velvety voice in person. Years since it had echoed in her thoughts.

Even though she'd half expected him to be here, it didn't lessen the impact of finally coming face-to-face with Gabe.

He was still trim and his face had matured attractively into that of a man. His smile curved in a jaw that was more defined, his hair was as lush and thick as it ever was. He'd always been good-looking. Now he was strikingly so.

Ever since Emily learned Gabe had been calling her, she'd been fantasizing about how she'd act if they should meet. She wanted to exude a cool, professional, I've-been-over-you-for-years attitude.

She got cool, all right. Frozen, in fact. All she could do was stare at him, her hand still outstretched for the file. And when she forced herself to finish the action, she looked down and saw that the folder trembled in her hand. She tossed the folder on the conference table.

He was staring at her. She could feel his dark-eyed gaze. Pasting a smile on her lips, Emily raised her eyes determinedly. "Hello, Gabe."

A corner of his mouth quirked upward as he reached the table. "How are you, Emily?"

She quickly held out her hand when it looked like, horror of horrors, that he intended to kiss her on the cheek. They may have a history, but this was business and she didn't want him to undermine her credibility in front of the others.

Smiling wryly, he shook her hand, giving it an extra squeeze, which she ignored.

"Good to see you again, Gabe."

"Is it?" he murmured. "You never returned my calls."

"No, I didn't. Though if you'd indicated it was business, I would have."

His smile dissolved and...was that a flash of hurt in his eyes?

"Ouch," he said softly.

Emily had no sympathy for him whatsoever. Whatever he was feeling now was one tiny, miniscule part of the hurt she'd felt when he'd left her. "When I heard the word 'biosphere,' I suspected that you'd be involved somehow."

That was probably why he'd called. He must have known that she was working for EduPlaytion and simply wanted to find out if she would be at the meeting. Perhaps his calls were only a courtesy alert that they might be coming face-to-face.

That possibility *did* give her conscience a prick or two, which went away at his next words.

"If you suspected I'd be here, then I'm surprised you came at all."

She *had* hurt him. The realization brought her no pleasure. "Professionally, it's a huge opportunity for me. And you, of all people, know how important these once-in-a-lifetime career opportunities are."

Emily wished she hadn't added that last part. Being spiteful wasn't like her at all and it certainly wasn't professional.

She started to apologize, but Gabe was hailed by

a man standing next to a slide projector. He turned away without another word.

That went well, Emily thought, disgusted with herself. She'd wanted to prove he meant nothing to her.

Instead, she'd proved the opposite.

"If everybody will take a seat, we can get started." A young fashionably bespectacled man stood with Gabe by the projector.

"Martin, I'd like to introduce Emily to everyone before we begin the presentation," Gabe interrupted, flashing his Gabe smile at the room. "Emily is the attorney for EduPlaytion. Emily, Martin Rimmer is with NASA public relations."

Emily nodded as Gabe indicated two more members of the PR team, which told her this project was even more important than she'd first assumed.

"This is Larry Ciner, president of Nutritional Engineering," Gabe continued.

Okay, *real* important.

Gabe introduced the rest of the table and Emily smiled blindly at them all. If this project was so important, then *why* hadn't there been more time to get ready?

"Jerry, EduPlaytion's head of technical development, is on his way over with the sample sketches we put together since we were told about the meeting this morning." Emily wanted it known just how much time they'd been given to prepare. The entire technical development department had been frantically working so EduPlaytion wouldn't come to the meeting empty-handed.

In fact, just as Emily finished speaking, there was a knock on the door and a flushed Jerry, laden with easel and portfolio, spotted her and hurried over to the table.

"You must be Jerry," Gabe said affably as Jerry took the seat next to Emily. "Just in time for the presentation."

"I thought that was what *I* was doing," Jerry remarked, smiling, even though Emily knew he'd been working flat-out for hours.

"We didn't expect you to have preliminary sketches for toys already," Martin, the PR man, told him. "We want you to see the presentation first."

Now they tell us. Emily and Jerry exchanged looks and Emily could swear she heard his teeth grind together.

Gabe picked up a remote control and dimmed the lights, then turned on the projector. "This is the same show we just gave the press."

So the media knew more than she did. Emily resolved to find out who exactly was in charge and have a little chat with him. In the meantime, she turned her attention to Gabe, remembering countless other occasions when she'd sat in an audience and listened to him lecture.

"I'll be leading the three biosphere teams," he told them as the first slide flashed on the screen. "And will be living in Bio 1, myself."

He must be so pleased, Emily thought automatically, and she was irritated with herself for thinking so. Gabe was far, far in her past. His dreams and ambitions were no longer any of her concern.

She'd cared once, but no more.

But as he continued to speak, Emily was helplessly aware of all the old feelings for him stirring again. She'd thought they were dead, but they'd only been dormant, like the seeds from the desert plants that waited for a rare rain to bring them to a short, but colorful life.

Listen to yourself. You're even thinking like him again.

But it was hard not to. Slide after slide showed three separate biospheres, one, built on an abandoned drilling platform in the Gulf of Mexico, would use marine resources for fertilizer and food. A second was located on the North Slope of Alaska. Gabe's was the sphere located in the Arizona desert. He liked to experiment in heat and arid conditions, she remembered.

She could hear the excitement in his voice and found she was still attracted to the passion he felt about his work. At one time, she'd erroneously thought that passion extended to her. At one time she'd thought they would have been celebrating their anniversary with Freddie and Hunter.

At one time, she'd thought she'd be a mother by now. A mother to Gabe's children.

Emily bit her lip, the physical pain helping her counter with the emotional one.

How could she have any child without thinking of Gabe and what might have been?

It didn't matter how long it had been since they'd seen each other, Emily knew. Gabe would always be a part of her.

She felt weak with the realization—weak and unable to cope with the rest of the meeting. She didn't feel able to cope with Gabe, either, but she would. In fact, seeing him in action again, remembering how he put his work before all else might destroy her feelings for him, just like the hot desert sun destroyed...oh, for pity's sake.

She would get over him. She *would*.

If they'd stayed married, she would have always been competing with his work, she reminded herself. And their children...

Unexpectedly, hot tears stung her eyes as Emily imagined missed soccer games, school plays and music recitals.

She'd done the right thing by ending their short-lived marriage.

She had.

Really.

The lights came up as the project logo appeared on the screen and Emily quickly brushed at the corners of her eyes, then smiled determinedly as Gabe's eyes sought hers, just as they always had at the end of a presentation.

His return smile jolted her. It was a tender, sentimental smile at a time when Emily didn't want to feel tender or sentimental. She wanted to feel strong, competent and in control.

Jerking her gaze away from his, she gave her attention to the NASA PR representative.

"We are pleased to have come to an agreement with EduPlaytion for a line of educational toys and science classroom aids that will mirror the experiments in the biospheres. I have to tell you, according to our focus groups, science teachers everywhere are going nuts over this.'' Martin gestured with his hands. ''Wish we'd thought of it sooner.'' He chuckled, but stopped when he was met with nothing but polite smiles.

''Thanks to the PR department, the public is interested in the biosphere project and I don't need to tell you,'' he added, and proceeded to tell them all anyway, ''that when the public is interested, the funding doesn't dry up. One way to keep the public interested is with these toys. That's our goal. We're here today to plan how to meet that goal. Now, Emily, if you could talk us through a typical EduPlaytion commercial tie-in in terms of what your company will provide contractually, we can brainstorm some marketing, products, and publicity from our end.''

Emily stood, glad that this was a subject she knew. Glad she'd appear competently professional in front of Gabe.

Conscious of his dark gaze on her the entire time, she hit the major points of a typical contract. ''But this is our boilerplate contract,'' she concluded, ''I'll have to meet with my counterparts at NASA and Nutritional Engineering to finalize the details for each product.''

''You bet you will,'' the Nutritional Engineering lawyer said with a grin.

''I look forward to it,'' Emily replied with an answering smile, hoping that he wouldn't insist on a meeting immediately following this one.

After Emily answered a few questions, Jerry presented his sketches, which prompted a volley of suggestions for additional toys or modifications to the ones he'd proposed.

When they began discussing possible timetables, Gabe intervened. "Martin?" Gabe's voice cut through the discussion. "If we're finished here, I say let the lawyers go and you people can stay and brainstorm all you like."

Escape! Emily exhaled in relief when Martin waved them away. She didn't know how much longer she could pretend to be unaware of Gabe's unrelenting gaze upon her. She was surprised the others hadn't noticed. Or maybe they had.

As she exchanged cards with the other lawyers, she felt Gabe waiting behind her.

"Let's get some coffee," he murmured next to her ear as she closed her briefcase.

"It's too hot for coffee."

"Then order one of those mocha icy slushy drinks. You know the kind." He took her arm, drawing her away from the others.

Pulling away would draw attention. "Don't you have to stay at the meeting?"

"I've heard enough to know the gist of things. Whatever they plan to do is fine with me as long as they understand that I have my own priorities—which is making sure this project is a success. Anything else comes second."

"Same old Gabe," Emily said, hearing the bitterness in her voice.

He didn't reply, but continued ushering her toward the door.

"Do I have any choice at all about this?"

"You can order coffee however you like."

"I meant about coming with you."

Gabe looked down at her, a smile curving his lips. "No."

Emily had only been protesting for the sake of protesting. She hadn't expected to walk away from the meeting without a private chat with Gabe.

She only hoped she could keep from revealing the feelings—both good and bad—she still felt for him. It was pointless to feel anything for him at all. Even now, he'd made it clear that his work came first.

They said little until they reached the hotel's coffee shop, which gave Emily time to recover her equilibrium as much as it was going to recover in Gabe's presence.

She ordered the largest, sweetest, caffeine-loaded drink on the menu.

Gabe ordered a plain cup of coffee. Black.

They carried their coffees over to a round, faux marble-topped table that was much too tiny for Emily's peace of mind. Sitting on an uncomfortable wrought-iron chair, she swallowed a large mouthful of her drink and waited for the sugar and caffeine to kick in.

Wearing the faintest of smiles, Gabe watched her over a cup of coffee as black as his eyes.

Emily took refuge in another swallow.

"How have you been, Emily?"

How had she been? Is that all he had to say—

How had she been? "Today in particular, or the past few years?"

Holding his cup in both hands, Gabe was in the process of bringing it to his mouth. After taking a sip, he carefully set the cup down, turning it until the hotel logo was facing him, then leaned on his elbows. "Let's start with today."

Emily didn't see the need to start at all. Her emotions were all in turmoil, and there was Gabe, sitting across from her looking fresh, energetic and crisp, while she felt wrung-out and limp.

Very conscious that she was losing the I'm-above-taking-petty-jabs battle, Emily forced herself to laugh with casual unconcern—hoping it came across as casual unconcern and not a nervous cackle. "Today has been...a challenge."

"Not because of me, I hope."

"Not unless you were responsible for calling that meeting with four hours notice." Emily sipped her drink.

"The project is scheduled to begin in two weeks. I have a lot to do before then."

Emily's mocha latte iced coffee thudded to the table. "You *were* responsible for calling the meeting."

Gabe's expression didn't change.

"And I'll bet you were the one who insisted I represent EduPlaytion." The biggest opportunity of her career and *Gabe* was responsible for...setting her up to fail. "How *dare* you!"

"You wouldn't return my calls and I had to see you."

"Now you've seen me. Goodbye." Emily stood to leave, but Gabe clamped his fingers around her wrist.

Emily looked down pointedly.

"Stay." He released her. "Please."

Curiosity. Curiosity was all that made her sit again, Emily told herself. "So tell me how it is that you're able to call the shots."

"I own Nutritional Engineering."

Owned it? "I see." Hadn't she always expected him to be a success? "And you dangled a huge contract in front of my company, insisted that I handle it, then didn't give us enough time to prepare just so you could humiliate me?" She felt her eyes sting. "Wasn't twice enough?"

"Emily—no. It wasn't like that." He looked genuinely alarmed.

Emily almost believed him. "Do the others know?"

"Know what?"

"That the contract was contingent on me handling it?"

He looked into his cup. "My people know. Whether they've mentioned it to the NASA people, I can't say."

"Oh, great." Emily closed her eyes, remembering the stares and the grins, which now seemed more like sneers. Remembering how Gabe looked at her during the entire meeting. She opened her eyes. "You have placed me in an untenable position."

"I've given you a fabulous opportunity."

"Which everyone knows I haven't earned."

Emily could tell from his expression that he genuinely hadn't considered how his actions might have appeared to others. So what else was new?

He sipped at his coffee, then spoke carefully. "I assumed everyone would think I wanted you because you're very good."

Emily looked him right in the eyes. "Lucky for you, I am."

After thirty seconds in her company, Gabe realized Emily was blisteringly angry. She might even hate him.

What had he done to make her that way?

He knew how big the biosphere toy account was, especially if science teachers adopted some of the experiments into the school curriculum. He thought she'd be flattered if he found out he'd requested her. To him, it was a show of good faith, a peace offering.

And maybe a chance to…no.

Gabe studied Emily as though she were a beautiful, but unknown, specimen of plant that might be poisonous.

Dr. Weber was wrong. He shouldn't have contacted Emily. This encounter was going as poorly as that long-ago lunch. Perhaps worse. Emily wanted nothing to do with him.

After they finished their coffee, he'd say goodbye, then walk out of her life forever. At least he could tell Dr. Weber that he'd met with Emily and then make up some story about them growing apart during the time he was on the Sahara project.

It was probably the truth, anyway.

But he never would have believed it. He'd thought he and Emily had forged a connection that would withstand anything. *She'd* broken it. He hadn't.

He looked at the way she sat stiffly in the chair and the cold unfriendliness in her eyes. Broken it? She'd hacked it off and burned any traces.

"So this was why you called me?" she asked.

"This…and old times' sake."

"What about old times?" she asked with a pinched smile he hated.

"Our paths have crossed again. Did you expect me to ignore you?"

"Our paths crossed because you crossed them."

They stared at each other for a long moment.

Gabe found himself erasing the mental image he'd held of her for all these years, even after their divorce. The image of the sweetly shy girl who obviously adored him was replaced with one of a young career woman with a hard look in her eyes and bitterness around her mouth.

But the real Emily had to be in there somewhere. She had to be.

And he wanted to find her.

He gave her a slow smile, watching as she drank more of her coffee. "So, here we are. You married? Kids? You always wanted kids."

"No." Her hand visibly shook as she set her drink on the table. "No children."

That surprised him. She hadn't said whether she was married or not, but she wasn't wearing a wedding ring. He wondered if she'd kept the one he'd given her. He still had the one she'd given him.

She shoved her hands into her lap under the table and her eyes were bright when they met his. "What about you?"

"No, I never married. With the way I work, it's hard to find the time to date."

"I imagine it is."

Something was very wrong. Was she a widow? Or— "Em? What's going on? What happened?"

"Nothing."

He leveled a look at her. "Something."

"Nothing!" she snapped and grabbed for her drink. It was empty and she slammed the paper cup on the table.

"But you're upset. I know someth-"

"*Nothing happened!* That's what's wrong, Gabe. I'm thirty-two years old and I have no husband and no children! And that's all I ever wanted in life."

Her words echoed around the coffee shop. Out of the corner of his eye, Gabe saw several heads turn.

Emily's own eyes were squeezed shut and she looked as though she was holding herself together with difficulty. "I'm sorry." She spoke in a careful whisper. "I have a headache—"

"Did you eat lunch?" Gabe interrupted.

"No."

"That explains the headache. C'mon. Let's get you something to eat." He hoped she wouldn't put up a fuss because he didn't intend to take no for an answer.

CHAPTER FOUR

SHE'D never lost it in the courtroom—not once, even though she hated courtrooms.

But Gabe...having him ask about children, when *they* should have had children...it was too much.

Emily allowed him to lead her out of the coffee shop, across the lobby to the hotel restaurant, which was Italian.

Gabe scanned the menu posted outside, but when Emily would have gone in, he draped an arm over her shoulder and walked her away.

"Gabe," she protested, sounding pitiful even to her. "This is fine. I've got a long drive ahead of me."

"Where are you living now?"

She hesitated, but it was silly not to tell him. "Out west in Katy."

It was suburbia. Family territory. He gave her a curious look before pushing open the heavy glass door. "You do have a long drive, which is why we're going to a steak house about a block and a half away from here. You need protein. If you insist, they've got a great salad bar, and I can personally vouch for their baked potato soup, but I don't want you loading up on carbs and falling asleep on the drive home."

In spite of herself, Emily smiled. For some endearing reason, a thick steak had always been Gabe's solution to life's problems. It was odd considering his affinity for plants, but maybe not when she thought about it.

Still smiling, she chuckled and glanced over at him. "Some things never change," she said softly.

He gave her a wry look. "And some things do. Come on. The fresh air will do you good."

"Since when is downtown Houston known for fresh air?"

He laughed and after that, the tension between them lessened and had nearly disappeared by the time they reached the end of the block, turned the corner, and Gabe indicated at a restaurant with a red neon Longhorn steer wearing a Stetson ringed with green jalapeño peppers.

"Have you heard about the research being done with jalapeño peppers and cold viruses?"

"No, but I have a feeling I'm going to," Emily said.

"Hey, I don't want to bore you."

"You know," she admitted. "You never did. You always did make the weirdest stuff sound fascinating."

"What's weird about plants?"

"I'm not getting into that argument. Tell me about the peppers."

"Just that researchers discovered that eating peppers temporarily raises the body temperature and may kill off cold viruses before they get a chance to take hold."

"Wouldn't drinking coffee do the same thing?"

"There seems to be something in the pepper oil that works. Now you can start eating one with your morning oatmeal."

Emily made a face. "Lovely."

They were close enough to the restaurant to hear the country and western music sounding from inside. Gabe opened the door to a rough weathered-wood/ branding-iron type decor. The staff wore cowboy hats and red gingham shirts with blue denim jeans. A clump of fake bluebonnets and orange Indian paintbrush were stuck in a small bud vase on each table.

They ordered and nibbled on chips and salsa. Emily's headache had nearly disappeared by the time their dinner arrived. Maybe food *was* all she'd needed.

She ate a giant salad and a modest-sized fillet, feeling better and better. And the better she felt, the better Gabe looked. His tall, dark looks were striking enough that Emily noticed a few female eyes glancing over at him and lingering. The fact that Gabe was apparently unaware of how he appeared to other women had appealed to a younger, less self-assured Emily. Even an older, more wary Emily. And she liked his hair this shorter length. His ears showed.

He had attractive ears for a man.

Their conversation fell into a pattern that was familiar, yet new. Since they hadn't seen each other for years, it centered in the present, on movies they'd been to, their opinions on various restaurants in Houston, even dipping into politics. At times

Emily forgot that she was with Gabe and not on a first date that was going particularly well.

At times, she forgot they'd been married at all. Gabe had been her friend before he'd been her lover and she'd felt a loss even her friendship with Freddie couldn't fill.

She found herself wanting to share bits and pieces of her life with him and did so, as if the years and the hurt had never been. She even went so far as to talk about the various toys EduPlaytion thought would be the hits of the next Christmas season, forgetting the new connection between Gabe's company and hers.

"So what do they think about the chances of the biosphere toys?" Gabe naturally asked.

Ah, yes. The biosphere. A little of the glow left the evening.

"I can tell you that EduPlaytion never backs a project they think will be unprofitable."

"I hope so. I wasn't certain about the toy idea at first, but what better way to keep the public aware of what we're doing than through the schools and their children?"

"You sound like you're quoting from the press conference."

He grimaced. "Sorry. It's just that this is so important, Emily."

She'd seen that look on his face before. It was the beginning-of-the-project look, when Gabe was excited about all the new knowledge out there waiting to be discovered.

It was the same look that had been on his face when he'd left her on their honeymoon.

She swallowed, more determined than ever not to reveal her feelings. She just intended to bury them again, anyway.

''The timing could be better than beginning this whole thing during an election year. We don't want funding to dry up when a new congress is looking for ways to cut the budget. But there were construction delays with the biospheres, themselves. We got a whole batch of the metal framing calculated in meters instead of feet like the glass panels that were supposed to fit in it had been. One of the two had to be changed…''

Emily let him talk. She could tell that he'd been consciously avoiding running on about his work and had asked her questions about her life, so she figured he was due a reward.

Besides, she liked listening to him talk. She always had.

The thing about being with Gabe, was that he was always looking to the future and he made it sound so exciting and bright. She wanted to be a part of that excitement—to watch him make things happen.

And she'd wanted her children to inherit that same sense of wonder and drive.

The good looks wouldn't hurt, either.

Gabe was talking, gesturing with his hands, when the waitress appeared. Without waiting for her to ask, he ordered coffee for both of them, and kept right on talking.

Emily settled in her chair, getting as comfortable

as she could on the vinyl cushion with the wooden ladder back, and surrendered to Gabe's spell once more.

In doing so, she was transported back to the time in the weeks before their marriage and with a sense of déjà vu realized that she might have heard some of this conversation before—maybe when her mind was full of wedding details and future plans of her own. Only that time, Gabe had been talking about another big project.

How could she have ever thought he wouldn't have wanted to go? Did she really think she, alone, was enough to hold his interest?

How naive she'd been. And how much in love.

Still in love.

She admitted it silently to herself, making sure she was occupied with stirring sugar into her coffee so Gabe wouldn't see the love in her eyes.

Letting it out instead of fighting it brought her a little relief. She could rest a few seconds before hiding her feelings from Gabe once more.

There was no shame in loving Gabe, she decided. They simply had different priorities in life. The problem was that he was doing exactly what he wanted to do and she wasn't.

But that was going to change, she thought, hiding her smile behind her coffee cup. Tonight, she was going to seriously study her profile booklets— maybe even make her choice. She'd already marked the most promising donors....

And they were all like Gabe.

Freddie was right and Emily hadn't seen it until

now. But she'd always felt he'd be the perfect father for her children. He had all the characteristics that she lacked. Gabe was outgoing, Emily was shy. He was ambitious and she would be just as happy as a homebody.

Why couldn't he be the donor?

The thought made her heart pound.

From her research, she'd learned that directed donors, as Gabe would be, had to pass the same screenings as all other donors, which included six months of health tests. Because of the biosphere, she knew Gabe had been rigorously screened, so she knew he'd be accepted as a donor—if he would, and Emily wasn't all sure he would, even if she could bring herself to suggest the idea.

But he'd be perfect. He was going to be gone for two years and it was unlikely that she'd be falling in love again anytime soon. Besides, she'd rather have his child than some stranger's.

She'd always wanted his child. A little brown-eyed curly headed boy. Or girl.

"You love your work, don't you?" she asked softly, when Gabe paused to drink half of his probably lukewarm coffee so the hovering waitress could refill his cup.

"I do." He looked at her, then smiled wryly.

"I always thought you'd have made a great teacher."

"Did you?" He considered it. "I've had plenty of student interns working with me before, but I'd go crazy if I had to spend all my time in a classroom. I want to be out there—" he gestured with a

sweep of his hand that threatened the plastic bluebonnets in the centerpiece "—making the discov-
eries that end up in the textbooks, not repeating
someone else's."

Even though what he did and what he wanted no
longer affected her, Emily could feel herself getting
caught up in Gabe's vision. "Since you own
Nutritional Engineering, then how is it that you're
able to go off and lock yourself up in a biosphere
for two years?"

Gabe learned forward. "That was the whole
point. I hire good people. I like doing things my own
way and I like field research. A few years ago, I was
getting too caught up in corporate politics and wast-
ing too much time justifying what I do and how I
do it, so I worked a deal and ended up with the
company."

He made it sound so simple. "And all so you
could continue your research?"

He nodded. "Basically."

Emily sat back in her chair. "I'm impressed. You
have the life you always wanted."

"Pretty much."

And she didn't. But she was about to change all
that, wasn't she? "So you're determined to stick this
biosphere thing out for two years?"

"Oh, yes," Gabe answered without hesitation.

"It's the most important thing in your life."

He laughed. "Right now, it's the only thing in
my life."

And she believed him. The more Emily talked
with Gabe and sensed his commitment to the proj-

ect—not that she ever doubted it—the more she thought about asking him to be the donor father for her child. The circumstances were too perfect.

Too perfect. As in why had he come back into her life at just this time? And the fact that he wasn't going to stay in her life.

So, could she raise Gabe's child without him?

But it wouldn't be Gabe's child. It would be *her* child, the way any other donor's child would be.

"Why *did* you want to see me, Gabe?" she asked, interrupting whatever he'd been talking about.

"It has to do with the project."

Of course it did. Everything he did was connected to one project or another.

"Just because I own the company doesn't mean I can't avoid the rules and regulations. The insurance company won't cover us unless the entire team has been screened and that includes me."

"You mean health screening?"

"Yes." He scowled. "Physical and mental."

"So...you need somebody to vouch for you, or something?"

Gabe looked distinctly put out. "In a way." He shifted and leaned forward. "You see, Em, this doctor I'm seeing thinks that I have *issues* with you. Unresolved issues."

Emily felt a variety of emotions. Sympathy was not one of them. Clearly, he blamed her for whatever disagreements he was having with his doctor. She was impacting his precious project and he resented it.

"And what issues might those be, Gabe?"

"About our marriage."

"And what marriage might *that* be, Gabe?" Emily bit off the words.

He had the audacity to look surprised and wounded. "Emily?"

"We were married for five days, Gabe."

"We were married for over two years!"

"We were legally connected for over two years. What we had was not a marriage."

"It was to me." He sounded so sincere. So cluelessly sincere.

"Really." Emily indicated that the waitress could refill her coffee. "Tell me about your idea of marriage."

"You sound like Dr. Weber."

"Then I like her." She stirred sugar into her coffee. "Do you avoid answering her questions, too?"

He stared at her, as though she were a plant who'd mutated. Emily sipped her coffee and waited. She figured she might as well drink as much coffee as she wanted, since she doubted she'd be able to sleep anyway.

"Marriage is when two people agree to build a life together."

"*Together,* Gabe. We were together five days."

"*Build* Emily. We were each building our future."

"But were we building the *same* future?" she asked quietly.

He stared at her. "I thought we were. Obviously, we were in different fields, but we were taking advantage of opportunities to further our careers."

"We weren't furthering our marriage. There was no sharing, no daily give and take."

"I'll concede that communications weren't the best—"

"They were virtually nonexistent."

"—and at the time I didn't anticipate that I would be unable to return—"

"Just how hard did you try to get back to the States, Gabe?"

"It wasn't as easy as you seem to think—"

"Two years?"

He frowned. "If you would let me finish a sentence, our discussion might bear fruit."

"Oh, goody. Plant humor."

Gabe's face was great. He was obviously so surprised that she wasn't little, wimpy Emily anymore.

You aren't being a very nice Emily right now an inner voice said.

Pooh. Look where being nice got her. "You want to talk plant, Gabe? I'll talk plant. What happens when you put a seed in the ground, water it and give it sunlight for a few days, and it sprouts and then you put it in a closet and never water it again? It withers and *dies*."

"Actually, Emily, we've developed plants that would complete their growth cycle under those circumstances."

She should have known. Emily gazed at the man across the table from her—the man who would have made the ideal father for her children. Assuming he never had anything more to do with them.

No. She was all upset. Even now, Gabe still didn't

get it. He never would and Emily knew that for her own peace of mind, she shouldn't have anything more to do with him. And the sooner she left, the better.

Finishing her coffee, Emily looked at her watch, then stood and held out her hand. "It was great seeing you again, Gabe. I look forward to doing a good job for you on this toy project. I imagine you'll be hearing progress reports from time to time, but if you ever have any questions, please give my assistant a call."

He hadn't taken her hand. "Emily, for God's sake, sit down."

She withdrew her hand. "Goodbye, Gabe. Good luck on your project." She started walking away from the table.

"Emily, wait."

Wait? Hadn't she waited long enough? She kept walking.

Gabe caught up with her by a giant bowl of peppermints in the reception area.

"Emily."

She stopped only to avoid a scene.

"I want you to come with me to my next session with Dr. Weber."

"Why?"

"Because she's going to ask me questions I can't answer, but I think you can."

"What questions?"

"Questions like what happened to us, Em?"

Emily stared at him. His brown eyes were full of sincerity and she didn't think it was faked. And then she glanced around the reception area of the busy restaurant. The band had just returned from its break and she and Gabe were already talking louder than she felt comfortable doing, especially considering the personal nature of their discussion.

"Why didn't you ask years ago?" *When it might have made a difference.*

"Because I didn't see it coming, Em. I honestly didn't."

She almost felt sorry for him. "You didn't see anything, period. You weren't here."

After another moment of searching her face, he said abruptly, "Come with me to see Dr. Weber."

"Why should I?"

He touched her arm, but at her expression allowed his hand to drop away. "I think she can help you."

"Help me? Aren't you the one being analyzed?"

"Screened and evaluated," he corrected.

"Whatever." Emily was weary of the discussion. Why didn't he just drop it? "What difference could it make now, anyway?"

"Emily, you're angry and you've been angry for the past ten years."

Emily rolled her eyes and headed for the door, pushing it open. The humid night air brushed against her, making her skin sticky after the air conditioning. "Gabe, I say this, not to be sarcastic, but in all sincerity—the world does not revolve around you or your projects. You have overestimated the importance our brief marriage had in my life."

"You're lying. I know you're lying. I don't know why, though."

She gave him a dry smile and began walking back to the hotel garage. "So you're saying the world *does* revolve around you?"

"You know I'm not."

"Sounds like it."

He was silent and Emily could see him thinking.

"You know, Em, there's a real chance that I won't be passed by Dr. Weber."

"Oh, come on! You own the company, for pity's sake!"

"I've told you that makes no difference. But, I have to say, if I'm not personally involved, my company won't be, either. And if that happens, the project is pretty much finished. There wouldn't need to be any toy tie-in. That would free up a lot of your time, wouldn't it?"

Emily stopped abruptly. "You rat, you're blackmailing me!"

"Not exactly—more like graymailing you."

"Oh, please." Still, Emily had to consider what he'd said. Gabe had always been clever about getting what he wanted. If she called his bluff and by the remotest chance something happened to cancel her company's contract...

They rounded the corner. The hotel was in sight. Emily walked faster.

"If I'm not involved with the biospheres, I'm guessing that some other firm would step in, since they're all built, however, they wouldn't be bound by any contracts we signed with EduPlaytion and may well want to find their own company."

They reached the hotel garage. "Oh, stop. Just

stop.'' Emily dug in her purse for her ticket and handed it to the valet. ''I'll come with you to see your doctor, not that I understand why, or what good it will do.''

A smile, his infamous Gabe smile, creased his face. ''Thanks, Em. You're the best.''

And then as though it was the most natural thing in the world, Gabe kissed her.

It wasn't a peck on the cheek, either, but a definite and thorough kiss.

One that gave Emily a lot to think about—when she could think again. At the moment his lips touched hers, her emotions had a complete meltdown. This was Gabe—she'd always been attracted to him. But they were no longer married—how could she feel such a strong response to a very public and unexpected kiss?

He tasted the same, he felt the same, she fit against him the same, the angle of their heads was the same.

But nothing *was* the same.

CHAPTER FIVE

"HELLO, Emily. I'm Dr. Weber. Thank you for coming today."

Gabe watched as the two women shook hands. Fortunately, Dr. Weber had come from behind her desk and led them over to a cushy sofa and chair area, so Emily was spared sliding in the slick leather chair.

Emily was smiling at the doctor.

She hadn't smiled at *him* today.

Come to think of it, the doctor hadn't, either, and he got the distinct impression that they were ganging up on him.

Well, maybe it was good that Emily and Dr. Weber had established a rapport.

Before Dr. Weber had started delving into his past relationship with Emily, Gabe had shoved it into the back of his mind. Now that he'd impulsively involved her with the biosphere project, he would no longer be able to do so. If Emily harbored resentment toward him, and it was clear that she did, then they'd better hash it out now so Gabe could take his lumps and they could all move on.

Are you sure you want to move on?

Emily was wearing a very unlawyerlike suit in a yellow color. She looked good. Darned good. But he'd always been attracted to her, so that shouldn't surprise him.

And, whether he wanted to or not, he *was* moving on. Clearly, she already had.

Emily and the doctor had been chitchatting and Gabe hadn't been paying attention. He needed to and it wasn't like him to be distracted when he needed to focus.

It must be Emily's perfume. The scent was a different one than she used to wear. The other one had been a floral type and Gabe could identify the essences of the flowers used in it.

This one...he inhaled. No flowers. It smelled good, though.

"Emily, I'd like you to tell me how you and Gabe met."

How they *met?* Hadn't he told the doctor already? Gabe tamped down his impatience. It was going to be a long afternoon if they were going over old ground.

"At school," Emily replied. "He was the lab assistant for one of my classes."

"And you dated all through school?"

Emily nodded.

"Did you have many boyfriends, Emily?"

"No. I was relatively shy and after Gabe—" she glanced over at him "—well."

Dr. Weber glanced at him, too, as though trying to figure out what Emily had seen in him.

"And you, Gabe?"

"I had no boyfriends at all. That's a joke," he added when neither woman smiled.

"Do you find this session a joke, Gabe?"

Did the doctor *always* have to repeat their names? "No, but I think that if we check our sense of humor at the door, we're not going to get anywhere. I understand that you are asking about past relationships. I didn't really have any. I mean, I had girls who were friends, but no one like Emily."

"And neither of you ever remarried?"

Gabe just looked at Dr. Weber. This, too, was old ground.

Emily shook her head.

"May I ask why not?" Dr. Weber addressed her question to Emily.

"You may ask, but I reserve the right not to answer."

"Fair enough."

"I don't think it's fair," Gabe interjected.

They both looked at him.

"I'd like to know why she never remarried."

Nobody said anything, making him feel uncomfortable. He suspected that it was deliberate and, therefore, resolved not to let his emotions be manipulated by either the doctor or Emily.

"Why do you want to know?" Dr. Weber asked.

"Curiosity. She used to talk about having kids." There was that look on Emily's face again. Gabe wished he could figure it out. Maybe Dr. Weber could. She was certainly studying Emily at the moment.

"Have you always wanted children?" she asked.

"Very much," Emily answered.

Even Gabe could hear the emotion in her voice.

He continued to listen as Dr. Weber drew Emily out about her desire for children and how she'd visualized their marriage and her role in it.

The more he listened, the more astounded he was. This wasn't what she'd wanted when they'd married. Sure kids, someday, but to hear Emily talk, she'd just wanted to be a housewife with a whole bunch of children. The life she described as being the one she wanted was nothing like the life she had now.

"You never told me any of this," Gabe finally said.

"You knew I wanted children."

"But...Em, there's a huge difference."

"I agree," Dr. Weber said to Gabe's surprise and then, "Gabe, answer the same question. How did you envision life after you married?"

Gabe knew a trick question when he heard one, but decided to answer honestly anyway. "I figured I'd get a job somewhere and I, naturally, hoped I'd enjoy what I did for a living. No, I didn't anticipate being gone for the first years of our marriage."

Emily listened to Gabe answer the same question that had found her revealing more than she'd intended.

She wanted to leave. By now it should be apparent to even the densest person—which Gabe was giving a pretty good imitation of being—that they'd been mismatched from the start.

No matter how much they'd loved each other.

Gabe loved his work more than anything and was incapable of understanding why others didn't find it as compelling as he did. He couldn't help it. He was just being Gabe.

"She *told* me to go!"

Emily hadn't been listening but immediately knew what they'd been discussing.

She saved the doctor from asking the next logical question. "But I didn't think you would."

"What?" Gabe was looking at her as though she'd lost her mind.

And after all this time, Emily wondered if she hadn't. "It was our honeymoon."

"Then why—"

"Then why did I tell you to go? Because I didn't want you to blame me for your lost opportunity."

"I wouldn't have blamed you!"

"Eventually you would have."

"Did you hear that?" he asked the doctor. "How logical is that? She was mad at me for something I hadn't even done yet."

"You'd been thinking about the project the entire time we were on our honeymoon." Emily remembered her feeling that something was between them—that they didn't have the same spark, the same soul-blending, that Freddie and Hunter had. "I think you already resented me."

"I made a couple of phone calls to talk to my friends before they left on a project that I'd made the subject of my master's thesis, and you're calling that resentment?" He looked at the doctor. "I'd already spent a year of my life researching details and working with the university's botany department in planning and proposing the Sahara Project and I'm not going to make excuses for thinking about it while I was on my honeymoon.''

No, she hadn't lost her mind. In fact the only thing she'd do differently was not marry him until he returned—if he would have.

That and not have listened to Freddie so much. Emily closed her eyes. She'd listened to *Freddie* more than Gabe.

"Emily?" the doctor prompted.

"Yes, I knew it was important to him—but he went along with the wedding plans. But, Gabe," she sighed and looked down at her hands. "If you had seen the look on your face when you realized you could go…I couldn't compete with that. And it was a good thing I didn't try. You left so fast. You left me on our *honeymoon.* You couldn't wait an extra week or two, oh, no. You left that afternoon. Can you imagine how humiliating that was? You—you—'' Her voice broke, but she forced the words out. "You didn't even make love to me again."

He looked as though he'd been turned to stone.

Emily could feel long-suppressed emotions churning toward the surface and knew she was headed for a bout of tears. "How much longer do I have to stay?" she asked Dr. Weber.

"I'm willing to continue the session as long as you wish, but you're free to leave at anytime, Emily.''

The good girl Emily would have stayed and seen it through. But honestly, she felt she'd given Gabe and the doctor plenty to discuss.

"Thank you. Then I'll leave now." She picked

up her purse and turned to Gabe. "Good luck on your project, Gabe." She shook the doctor's hand. "He truly is the best person for the job."

On the drive home, Emily turned the music on her car stereo up as loud as she could and sang along, thus avoiding breaking into sobs until she collapsed on her bed in her modest three-bedroom house in suburbia.

She hated him for doing this to her.

She hated everything about it. Hated revealing her longings and desires and the humiliating honeymoon in front of the doctor and in front of a Gabe who clearly hadn't had any idea.

Hated feeling as though she'd been wrong. She probably was totally responsible for the mess she'd made of her life, though there weren't many who'd agree that her life was a mess.

Mess was the wrong word. It was a great life, but it was the wrong life for her. It wasn't the one she wanted to be living.

After an hour of feeling sorry for herself, Emily decided that she'd wasted enough tears on Gabe. After all, it was due to him that she was making nearly twice the salary she'd made before. She could save plenty of money for hiring help when the baby came. By being involved with only one project at EduPlaytion, Emily envisioned being able to schedule days when she could work from home.

Yes, Gabe had actually helped her and maybe she should just concentrate on that and stop resenting him for what she didn't have. Hadn't she already started making plans for getting the kind of life she wanted? For having a baby?

Emily felt better, so she changed clothes, splashed cold water on her face and fixed herself a sandwich, along with a glass of milk. Couldn't start too early stockpiling calcium. Turning on the television to the local news, she sat on her sofa and thumbed through the donor catalogs while she ate and half-listened to the news.

There was a knock on her front door. One of the kids next door had probably thrown his basketball over her fence. She got up to answer the door and was completely astounded to find Gabe standing there, hands shoved into his pockets.

"Hi, Em."

And still, *still* her pulse quickened and she felt that inner awareness she'd always felt when she saw him or heard his voice. "How did you know where I lived?"

"I read your address when you filled out the form in Dr. Weber's office."

Emily remembered wondering why she had to fill out the form when she wasn't a patient, but the receptionist had explained that it was to protect both her and the doctor. Emily now wished she'd asked what it would protect them from. Certainly not Gabe. "You were sitting across from me. You mean you read it upside down?"

"Yes."

He must have really wanted to know where she lived.

Gabe took a step forward and before she could

stop herself Emily backed up and then it seemed stupid not to move to the side and let him come inside.

He was going to anyway.

While Gabe glanced around the main living room, Emily walked to the sofa, closed the donor catalogs and turned them over so he wouldn't know what they were.

He wandered toward the sliding glass doors that opened onto Emily's plant-filled patio. "This is nice."

"Thanks."

"Why did you move way out here?"

"Good schools." She looked up at him just then and felt a pang.

Behind him was her kitchen with the colors she'd picked herself and the easy-clean surfaces she'd chosen in anticipation of sticky handprints. It could have been their kitchen.

And there could have been sticky handprints instead of the pristine surfaces.

Right now, Gabe could have been coming home from work and their children could be clinging to his legs, happy to see their daddy.

Who was she kidding? Gabe wouldn't have worked normal hours.

"Good schools are a selling point for you?" he was saying.

"Yes." Emily didn't offer any further explanation and Gabe didn't ask. "Would you care for some iced tea?"

"Sure. Thanks."

Emily walked into the kitchen, uneasily watching through the bar area to see that he'd gone to sit on her sofa. What if he decided to leaf through the booklets on her coffee table?

But Gabe had noticed her half-eaten sandwich. "I've interrupted your dinner. Sorry."

"I can fix you a sandwich, too, if you like." Why did she offer to do that? She wanted him to leave before they started having a discussion she didn't want to have.

"A sandwich would be fantastic." Looking utterly weary, he leaned his head back and covered his face with his hands.

Emily had only cooked for Gabe once before. She and Freddie had planned an elaborate meal featuring flaming baked Alaskas at the end because they sounded so elegant and difficult, Gabe and Hunter were sure to be impressed.

Baked Alaskas weren't that hard to make—or they shouldn't have been, but Emily had raised the oven rack to broil garlic bread and Freddie had shoved the desserts into the oven without lowering the rack first. Meringue stuck to the heating element and burned, smoking up the kitchen and making a horrible stench.

Emily had never cooked a complete meal for Gabe by herself. She'd never had the chance. She spread mayonnaise on two slices of whole wheat bread. This hardly counted.

Gabe opened his eyes when she carried his sandwich into the room. "Thanks. I know you were just being polite in offering, but I'm wrung out after this afternoon.''

He was wrung out?

''Why did you come here?'' But she already knew.

''To talk.'' He bit into his sandwich and downed half his glass of tea. Carefully setting the glass in a coaster, he said, ''If I'd known how things were going to turn out, I wouldn't have gone to the Sahara.''

''If I'd known how things were going to turn out, I wouldn't have told you to go—no, that's not true.'' If ever there was a time for blunt honesty, this was the time. ''If it hadn't been that project, it would have been another. It's better that I found out early.''

His face hardened. ''You make me sound like a complete jerk. I *married* you. I expected to live with you and make a life together. Did you think I'd just park you in a house somewhere and take off and do my own thing?''

Instead of answering, Emily bit into her sandwich.

''For pity's sake, Em! You went to law school. What would it have been like if I'd stuck around? You would have felt guilty because you should have been studying instead of spending time with me.''

She gave him a direct look. ''I wouldn't have gone to law school.''

He gestured with his hands. ''There you are then.''

''I never wanted to go to law school.''

Gabe stared at her. ''Then—I don't understand.''

''I just said that about going to law school because you were looking for an excuse to leave without feeling guilty,'' Emily admitted.

"Is that what you've been telling yourself all these years?"

"It's the truth."

"Then why did you go to law school while I was gone? You could have done something else. We're talking three years, Em. You must have liked something about it."

It was a reasonable question, and one she'd asked herself. "School was hard work, and kept me from thinking about anything else too much." *Thinking about you.* "And, too, it's what Freddie and Hunter did. I didn't have any better ideas."

"Freddie." He gave a disgusted shake of his head. "Is she still bossing you around?"

"She doesn't boss me around."

He made a skeptical noise. "She directed our entire wedding!"

Emily's jaw dropped in outrage. "So that's your plan? Blame Freddie for everything that went wrong?"

"No, but for pity's sake, Em, we even went on the damn honeymoon with her! I'm surprised you didn't marry *her* instead of me."

"Hunter didn't have a problem with the double honeymoon," Emily said, offended.

"Did you ask him?"

"I assume he would have said something to Freddie if he objected."

Gabe drew a deep breath and let it out quickly. "I think you and Freddie do too much assuming."

Emily threw down the last bit of her sandwich. "Why did you follow me here, Gabe? Am I supposed to grant you absolution, or something? Is that it? Did you bring a paper for me to sign attesting to your complete blamelessness in the breakup of our marriage? Well, bring it out and let me sign it."

"Emily."

"I'm serious. Our divorce was entirely my fault. You did nothing wrong. There. Happy?"

"Of course not."

"What more do you want, Gabe?"

He stared at her a long time, so long, Emily felt tears threatening, and she wasn't about to cry in front of him if she could help it.

"I want you to be happy, Em."

"Then leave me alone!" she burst out.

"I can't leave you when you're like this."

Darn, she *was* going to cry. On the pretense of clearing away her plate, Emily got up from the sofa. Gabe reached for her wrist, his hand warm and steady. "Let me go," she whispered.

"No. Not until you tell me—"

A sob escaped. Emily covered her mouth with her hands, dropping her plate in the process. It shattered against the coffee table.

The broken plate didn't matter. Breaking into uncontrollable sobbing did.

Without a word, Gabe drew her next to him on the sofa, holding her against his chest as she cried.

Emily was aware of his hand gently stroking her hair and soothingly whispered words floating around her.

If she'd been able to talk to him like this before, then... The thoughts of what-might-have-been just made her cry harder.

"Emily...Emily, what did I do?"

"You made me fall in love with you!" With a heroic effort, Emily pulled herself out of his arms and grabbed for her napkin. "And now...you've come back and stirred everything up again. And I was just finally...and now you...I've never been able to fall in love with anyone else!"

"Neither have I."

"Don't say that! Don't you see what you've done?" Sweeping bits of broken plate and sandwich crumbs away, she grabbed for the donor catalogs and artificial insemination information. Flipping them over she slapped them down in front of him one at a time. "Look! All I ever wanted was children and now I have to resort to picking their father out of a catalog and raising them alone."

Gabe was shocked. Utterly and completely shocked. He'd never seen Emily cry, not like this. A few times her eyes got bright when she was happy or had seen a weepy movie, but nothing like this.

And then she shocked him again. He stared at the words on the booklets in front of him and still couldn't believe that Emily, of all people, was considering artificial insemination.

She wanted children. Obviously very much. And it was his fault that she didn't have any.

He looked at her sitting on the sofa, arms wrapped around herself in a classic pose of complete misery.

He felt horrible. Awful. Even a little sick. Dr. Weber was right. He did have unresolved issues with Emily. Guilt.

"Emily, I guess a part of me always knew that I shouldn't have gone to the Sahara, but I honestly thought you were willing to work and live apart for a while so we could skip the struggling-young-marrieds-living-with-box-furniture-in-a-tiny-apartment-with-thin-walls stage. We would have been financially set and so would our children."

"Children," she whispered and a tear trickled down her cheek.

"Yeah." Gabe found he had to swallow, himself. "College funds—private school if they wanted—designer tennis shoes—the works."

Emily's trembling lips curved upward but couldn't hold the smile. She bit back a sob. "They would have had your curly hair and dark eyes, I just know it." She met his eyes then, her own almost black with misery.

Gabe felt helpless with guilt and regret and an overwhelming desire to put things right. He picked up the catalog, imagining Emily making a selection and then going through the unemotional procedure alone. Sweet Emily. Sweet, traditional Emily.

And the cost—he blinked at the table of average expenses for the procedure and the fact that it wouldn't be covered by health insurance. "Oh, Em. Don't do this."

She closed her eyes then, but tears trickled out the corners. She impatiently wiped them away. "I'm grateful that modern medicine has given me this choice. This isn't a whim of mine, Gabe. I've been preparing for over a year. I'm ready to have a child,'' she said simply.

And he heard himself say, ''Then let me give you one.''

CHAPTER SIX

"WHAT?"

He couldn't have said that.

But Gabe reached for Emily's hands and held them, soggy napkin and all. "I want to father a child for you, Emily. Let me make up for all the hurt I've caused you."

Emily stared at him. He sounded so sincere and he was saying words she'd heard only in her dreams. "You can't just...it's a little more complicated than you think, Gabe."

A corner of his mouth twitched. "Not from what I remember."

"These banks have very strict screening procedures. Even directed donors go through a six-month health and psychological screening."

"I wasn't talking about going through a donor program and you know it. I was thinking we could make a baby the old-fashioned way."

Emily went cold and hot at the same time. She *hadn't* known it.

"Although to set your mind at rest," Gabe continued, oblivious to Emily's reaction, "I've already had a rigorous health screening and you've met my counselor."

"It's not my field, but I'm sure there are legal

100

issues, as well." How could she manage to sound so calm?

"I'll sign anything you want," he promised quickly.

His words echoed the ones she'd spoken earlier.

"You're not thinking this through, Gabe."

"Yes, I am. We've got all weekend. I'll stay here with you. If it's meant to be, then it'll happen. If not, then..." He picked up one of her catalogs. "You go this route."

He *was* serious.

A weekend. Gabe was willing to commit for an entire *weekend*. He wasn't offering to give up his project even if she became pregnant with his child. But the biosphere—oh, yes, he was willing to commit to an entire two years for that.

He probably looked on making a baby as just planting seeds of a different kind.

Emily began laughing hysterically.

"Emily!" He shook her a little.

"You—you—"

"I'm completely serious, Emily. Doesn't it make sense?"

The incredible thing was, it was possible that she could conceive. She'd been charting her temperature for the past three months and this was an opportune time.

And, and it was Gabe.

Gabe.

She could have Gabe's child.

Right in the middle of laughing, she started sobbing again.

"No..." He enfolded her in his arms. "I was trying to make you happy. Why can't I get it right?"

His voice was so filled with self-loathing that Emily bit her tongue with the effort of holding back more sobs. She wasn't normally like this, truly. She sat up intending to reassure him when she saw his face.

He was in agony, his eyes dark with pain as they searched her face. His fingers brushed a leftover tear from her cheek, his lips moved and she could see that he was mouthing her name over and over.

"Gabe." Smiling sadly, she touched his face. "It isn't up to you to make me happy. Please don't think that way."

"But I made you unhappy!" His voice cracked with emotion. "Emily I—"

And then he was kissing her and she was kissing him back, their mouths fused with long-suppressed emotion.

Emily couldn't even remember when the kiss began. Just one instant they were apart and the next they were together. She wasn't aware of who moved first, only that their kisses were feeding a hunger long denied.

It had been so long since he'd held her in his arms.

Emily forgot that she was a thirty-two-year-old lawyer and was instead that young college student with a huge crush on the cute lab assistant with the snapping black eyes and incredible enthusiasm for botany.

She'd studied hard so she could answer any question in class. She spent every spare moment at the lab hoping to find him there. More often than not, she did.

And then one afternoon when she was measuring growth and recording data—actually working for once and not looking for him—there he was, asking her for coffee.

He hadn't kissed her then, nor after any other of their coffee dates. They became a regular Friday afternoon standing date. And then a Wednesday afternoon one, too. No, Gabe had wanted to avoid any hint of impropriety, even though they were both students, and keep things casual until after the semester ended and Emily was no longer taking the course.

At the time, she didn't know this, though if she'd been more experienced she would have been able to figure it out. During the weeks of coffee dates and long conversations, Emily thought Gabe considered her only a friend, someone who shared his love of plants. Emily actually only liked plants because Gabe liked them; she could take or leave them the rest of the time. She'd returned for the spring semester wanting to take the next level of botany, but was disappointed to find it didn't fit in with her course schedule.

What excuse could she give for hanging around the lab anyway?

She was still unpacking the day she arrived when Gabe called her and invited her for a hamburger.

Emily would never forget the heart-pounding moments when she waited for him to pick her up. She hadn't seen him for six weeks. She remembered the way he took her hand as they walked down the steps of her dorm, something he hadn't done before. And then...and then, before opening the car door for her, he'd turned to her and said simply, "I missed you."

The look he gave her made the blood pound in her ears until she was light-headed. He stood close to her, staring intently with his dark eyes as his chest rose and fell in the cold January air.

She remembered the way he glanced all around them, then jerked open the car door. Emily slid across the cold vinyl seats and Gabe ran around the front of the car. The instant he was inside and the door slammed behind him, they were reaching for each other. And then he kissed her with the same incredible hunger with which he was kissing her now.

The explosive happiness of their first kiss mingled with the relief of finally touching him the way she'd wanted to for so long and knowing he felt the same way about her, was exactly how Emily felt in Gabe's arms right this minute.

It was a dangerously hungry happiness that was well on the road to heartbreak.

She hadn't known it then, but she knew it now.

Did the knowledge stop her from kissing him back?

No.

And it didn't stop her from falling against the pillows on her sofa with him on top of her, either.

Their sole conversation consisted of murmuring each other's name as though they had to convince themselves that they were finally together again.

Emily surrendered to his drugging kisses, letting the hurt stay in the past, allowing herself to enjoy the present.

"Emily, I love you," Gabe whispered fervently against her mouth.

And Emily knew he meant it—at this moment. That was what she hadn't understood before, that Gabe could love her, but love his work more. As long as she remembered that fact this time, she could accept what love he had to give.

As long as she didn't want more. And Emily vowed to protect herself from wanting more. Look at what she might get—a child conceived in love rather than a doctor's office.

Gabe's child.

Just remember to be satisfied with the love he has to give. Make it enough.

And so she whispered back, "Please give me a baby, Gabe."

He lifted his head and looked into her eyes. "I'm not going to ask if you're sure, because I know you are. You're going to be a wonderful mother, Emily. I'm honored that you want to have my child."

She could feel moisture leaking out the sides of her eyes and running down her temples into her ears.

"You're crying again," he whispered, using his thumbs to catch the drops.

"Happy tears, Gabe."

"Oh, Emily." He touched his forehead to hers, then kissing her lightly, he asked, "Do you want to go into your bedroom, or stay on this outstandingly comfortable sofa?"

"Stay." Emily was afraid moving would awaken her from the wonderful dream she was having. A dream in which Gabe murmured endearments, old and new, but which were all the sweeter. A dream in which she and Gabe were in their home.

A dream in which the past ten years had been the dream.

Gabe moved one of the pillows from against the back of the sofa and settled her against his arms so that they were both on their sides.

He kissed her lightly and frequently on her mouth, her cheeks and her forehead, and even her nose, which made her smile. Mostly, he spent long moments looking into her eyes, as he stroked her, forcing her to reconnect with him on a deeply emotional level.

As Emily gazed into his eyes, she felt as though she were fighting against an undertow, fighting to hold something of herself in reserve. She couldn't give her whole heart to Gabe again and survive.

But she could celebrate a time when she *had* given him her heart and thought she'd held his heart in return.

During their brief honeymoon, Emily had never taken the initiative in lovemaking. Now, as she gazed into his eyes, she also unbuttoned his shirt and ran her hands over his chest allowing him to see her enjoyment as her fingers smoothed over the taut skin.

Gabe's sharply indrawn breath told Emily how she was affecting him. She smiled and kissed his throat and down his chest as she drew the edges of his shirt apart.

"Emily…" Her name was a sigh.

Smiling, she sat up and tugged until he sat as well, then she drew his shirt off his shoulders.

"Oh." She just looked at him.

"What?" He glanced down at his chest.

"You have muscles."

"Yeah." He casually flexed his arm and shoulder.

"You didn't used to have muscles like that."

"I've been spending a lot of time shoveling dirt lately. The crew had to get identical flats prepared for the three biospheres and we had to formulate the appropriate growth medium and—"

Emily touched his mouth with her fingers. "Just let me enjoy the muscles, Gabe."

He flexed his arm again. "You go in for this sort of thing?"

"More than I thought I did." She ran her hands over his shoulders, feeling the strength in them, thinking how easily they could lift a laughing toddler high into the air.

Then she did something she never would have had the daring to do before: when Gabe leaned forward to kiss her, she shook her head and gave him a subtle smile as she unbuttoned her own stretchy knit top.

When she saw the expression on his face and the growing passion reflected in his eyes, she slowed her fingers, drawing out the task, making each tiny button slowly slide through the buttonhole.

Gabe swallowed and she saw the tendons in his

arms work and realized that he'd clenched and unclenched his hands. His eyes were fixed on the movements of her fingers.

Emily licked her lips and his gaze caught the tiny movement before returning to her fingers.

His breathing quickened, becoming shallower the closer to the last button Emily got.

She enjoyed this new feeling of feminine power and realized that play and teasing had been missing in their brief marriage. They'd been so new to each other and so young and so, well, *serious* about the business of making love. Now, when it *was* so serious, Emily felt like teasing Gabe.

Her fingers tugged at the last tiny button. "It's stuck," she said softly into the tense silence. She pretended to push and twist at it.

"Let me," Gabe said gruffly, nudging her fingers out of the way.

His fingers, the same ones that could transplant tiny seedlings without damaging their tender root systems, were now clumsy. They might have even been trembling the slightest bit.

Emily never knew for certain, because with a forceful, "Dammit!" Gabe jerked open her top and yanked it off, sending it flying across the room one way and the button the other. Emily heard the *plink* as the button hit something before falling to the floor to join the pieces of broken plate. Her bra followed, but Emily didn't see which direction it went.

Frankly, she didn't care. Gabe was murmuring incoherently as he pressed wildly urgent kisses against her mouth and neck and breasts.

Had he ever wanted her this desperately before?

Had *she* ever wanted *him* this desperately before?

"Emily, you're so beautiful. You were always beautiful. Waiting for you was so hard..."

Before she could analyze what he meant, Gabe was unsnapping the waistband of her khaki shorts.

Emily returned the favor, then stood and shimmied out of her shorts and underwear, watching as Gabe did the same.

They stood before each other with as much wonder as they had on their wedding night.

"You look...lusher," Gabe said finally.

"I hope that's not a synonym for fat."

Unsmiling, he shook his head. "Womanly, sensual...erotic."

She *felt* womanly, sensual, and erotic, along with a few other choice descriptions.

The new sensual Emily drew her hands down his body in frank appraisal, keeping her eyes on his the entire time and watching as his lids grew heavy with desire. "Do you want me, Gabe?"

"Yes," he whispered hoarsely.

Still smiling, she lay on the sofa and held out her arms in invitation.

Gabe covered her body with his, sighing into the crook of her neck as he did so. "You feel so good, Em," he murmured.

So did he.

Gabe took his time teasing her with kisses and touching her with gently stroking hands until Emily involuntarily moaned aloud, surprising herself.

She'd never been a moaner, but she'd apparently become one now.

Gabe was making love to her, not just making a baby with her. Emily felt obligated to tell him that he didn't have to, except that it felt so good she didn't want him to stop.

So she said nothing, other than the moans, which were soon accompanied by gasps and an occasional, "Oh, Gabe!"

She wanted to give him pleasure, too, and discovered that when she ran her hands down his back and cupped his hips, that his pleasure became hers.

"Emily, you amaze me," he murmured at one point, before kissing her deeply.

Emily matched his kiss, drawing his tongue deeply into her mouth the way she wanted to draw him deeply into her body.

He groaned and gasped, "Now, Em!"

"Yes!"

And once more, Emily was joined with Gabe, her one true love.

She didn't want him to be her one true love, but right now she'd just acknowledge that he was and deal with the hurt later. Being this close to Gabe again was worth it. Just as she had before, she knew that at this moment, Gabe was focused totally on her and not on a plant somewhere.

He was hers. Completely. Totally.

For now.

Instead of moving, Gabe continued to kiss her. Emily liked Gabe's kisses, but he'd never kissed her at this point in their lovemaking before and she was touched.

And then she felt his hand caress her breast with a deliberate insistence until she felt a warmth grow deep within her.

Only then did he begin to move.

To Emily's surprise, the warmth inside her continued to grow until she was matching Gabe's movements, unable to help herself. Each time she did so, she felt wound tighter and tighter until there was a sudden release and liquid fire raced through her veins.

"Oh, Gabe!"

At that moment Gabe found his own release within her. Emily clutched him closer as the echoes of her own pleasure faded away.

She didn't want this moment to end, ever.

Dangerous thinking, that. But maybe it wouldn't end. If there were any justice in the world, this act of momentarily perfect love and harmony would have conceived a baby and Emily could relive the moment each time she saw her son or daughter.

"Oh, please," she whispered.

Gabe drew his head until he could look at her. "Please what, Em?"

She smiled. "Please, can we do that again?"

Emily gave herself the weekend as a present. Until after Sunday evening dinner, she refused to think about the future and resolved to live only in the here and now with Gabe.

They might really have been married ten years,

so easily did they fall into a comfortable domestic routine.

While Emily put their plates and glasses in the dishwasher, Gabe vacuumed the shards of broken plate out of her carpet.

They found a movie on television that they'd both seen before but had liked. Emily popped popcorn into the microwave and they shared the bowl while they watched the movie from the same couch where they'd earlier made love.

When the movie was over, they both looked at each other. Without saying a word, they turned off the TV and lights and headed to Emily's bedroom.

Morning brought none of the awkwardness Emily dreaded. She awoke first, wanting to make a special breakfast. There was nothing special in her refrigerator, but she could manage French toast with powdered sugar and strawberries.

Emily set the table and put the sugar and strawberries in the center, brewed the coffee and made the mixture for the French toast.

It was still early, she supposed and she was wondering what to do with herself, when warm arms encircled her waist.

Gabe rested his chin on the top of her head. "Is that going to be French toast?"

Emily could feel the vibrations when he spoke. "Yes."

"And you haven't started it, yet, I see."

Emily turned on the stove burner. "I wanted it to be hot when you ate it."

Gabe reached from behind her and turned off the stove. "Why don't you hold off then?"

Taking her hand, he led her from the kitchen and back to the bedroom.

Breakfast became brunch and neither of them minded.

After eating, Gabe took his mug of coffee and stood by the back sliding glass doors, peering out at her yard. "You haven't done landscaping out here, have you?"

"I've only been in the house three months," she told him. "I figured that since the summers are so hot, I'd just wait and plant some things in the fall."

"What things?" he asked immediately.

"Oh, you know, green things. Things that make flowers." She'd walked into a trap.

"Any particular green things?" he asked as she'd known he would.

"Hardy green things."

"You know, Em," he said, thoughtfully. "There are all these new plants developed especially to withstand Houston summers. And you can't go wrong with Texas natives." He drained his coffee. "Come on. Let's find a nursery."

Well, Emily thought philosophically, they couldn't spend all their time in bed.

Gabe was in his element. He carefully inspected about a million plants, happily telling her which ones were complementary when planted beside each other.

She knew how they were going to spend their afternoon when Gabe couldn't stand it and rented the tiller and then loaded flats of plants into her trunk.

Emily had to make a trip home to unload while Gabe remained at the nursery and bought more plants.

It figured, Emily thought. They both wanted to spend time in nurseries.

The builder had put seven tiny bushes and a spindly tree in each front yard of Emily's neighborhood. Gabe had no compunction about yanking out the bushes and transplanting them along the side of the driveway.

"Will you look at this?" He gestured to the tightly compacted root ball that unearthed easily when he pulled. "These poor things were never going to have a chance. Come on guys. You'll be lots happier over here."

He left Emily digging holes for the azaleas while he mixed all sorts of nutrients into her soil.

When the temperature climbed into nineties during the afternoon, he discarded his shirt and slathered on sunblock.

From under her hat, Emily watched the play of muscles in his back and arms as he worked the tiller through the front beds. Shortly afterward, he went to work tilling new beds in the back.

Emily sighed. Planting impatiens just wasn't the same after that.

"I'm going to return the tiller," he called as he wheeled it down her driveway hours later. He loaded it into his car trunk and tied down the lid, then returned for his shirt.

"Not bad," he commented on her handiwork. "Don't forget to feed them iron for color."

Emily was feeling so happy that the remark didn't even bother her.

Gabe was gone a long time, long enough for Emily to wonder if he'd changed his mind and didn't intend to come back.

But he did, arms laden with shopping bags. "I got us steaks for dinner. Do you have a grill?"

Emily shook her head.

"Good. I bought one of those little ones while I was buying a change of clothes." He disappeared into the house.

Emily rocked back onto her heels. Gabe was going to grill steaks out on her patio after a Saturday spent working together in the yard. How much more domestic could they get?

Her eyes stung. *No. Enjoy now. Don't spoil it by wishing for more.*

She drew a deep calming breath and smelled the charcoal Gabe had lit.

She would enjoy now. She would.

Now turned out to be a lot of fun. Emily cleaned her gardening tools and put them in the garage. Sure enough, there on the patio was a small tabletop grill containing burning charcoal.

Seasoned steaks waited in butcher paper on the kitchen counter and she could hear the shower running in the bedroom.

Emily stretched. She wanted a hot bath to ease her sore back muscles. While she waited, she could make a salad and set the table.

She was looking through the vegetable crisper when Gabe found her.

"There you are. I've been waiting for you."

She straightened, and saw that he was wearing only a towel. "You were in the shower."

He grinned. "Where did you think I was waiting?"

"Gabe!"

He held out his hand.

"Gabe?"

"Emily?" His hand was still outstretched.

She took it.

The charcoal had burned to a white powdery ash by the time they returned to it and Gabe had to relight more.

Neither of them minded the delay.

It was late Sunday afternoon when they finished Emily's landscaping. This time, she followed Gabe into the shower.

Afterward, when they lay, all tangled arms and sheets, in Emily's bed, she held Gabe close and wouldn't let him pull away because she knew that when he did, it would be for the last time.

She inhaled deeply at the crook of his neck, searching beneath the clean soap smell for the scent of him, wanting to imprint the memory. Running her fingers lightly up and down his spine, she memorized every bump and ridge. She moved her cheek against the beginning roughness of his beard and finally just wrapped her arms around him letting his weight press her back into the mattress.

"Em?"

Emily swallowed and loosened her arms. "Yes?"

Gabe brushed his lips across her forehead, rolled to the side and gathered her against him, spoon fashion.

"You know, Em, I was thinking. I've got two weeks before I have to enter the biosphere—maybe more, if there are any delays. And to be honest, there usually are, especially with a project this big. So I might have as much as a month. Why don't I move in here with you?" He dropped a kiss on her shoulder. "More chances for you to get pregnant."

Emily had to consciously remember to breathe. She could do nothing about her racing heart. Gabe could probably feel it.

The moment she'd loosened her arms, she'd mentally told him goodbye. And now, he was offering her more time. A whole month. Maybe.

She'd been barely able to protect herself for two days. How could she handle a month? Emily closed her eyes, determined to squeeze back the threatening tears. "You said something on Friday. You said, 'If it's meant to be, it'll happen.' I'm going to stick with that."

He was silent for several moments. "Are you saying you *don't* want me to stay?" Clearly, he hadn't anticipated her refusal.

"That's right."

"But what if you aren't pregnant?"

"Then I'll choose a donor." It was a good thing Gabe couldn't see her face.

He said nothing for a long time, then, abruptly, he released her and pulled on his shorts.

Emily drew the sheet around her. If she didn't know better, she'd think he was hurt. "It's nearly seven...would you like me to call out for pizza?" It was an offer mostly to fill the silence.

"Uh, no. I'd better get going. I'll grab a burger somewhere." He shoved his arms through his shirt.

As he moved through her house gathering up his things, Emily quickly dressed. Within a couple of minutes, Gabe was standing at her front door, holding a paper bag from the local discount store with the clothes he'd been wearing Friday and that Emily had washed for him.

"Goodbye, Em." He leaned down, at the last minute kissing her cheek rather than her mouth. "You'll let me know, won't you?"

Emily nodded tightly. "As soon as I know anything."

He stared at her a moment, looking as though he wanted to say something else, then smiled and said only, "I hope everything works out for you, Em."

"Thanks. So do I."

And then he was gone.

CHAPTER SEVEN

GABE had driven halfway back to his furnished rented apartment before the fact that Emily hadn't wanted him to stay fully sank in.

He hadn't wanted to leave. He hadn't expected to leave. He and Emily had been great together. In fact, the past two days ranked right up there with the best days of his life.

He couldn't believe that she'd been as responsive as she had and then just said goodbye when they'd been right in the middle of a...second honeymoon.

Honeymoon. *Honeymoon.* And that's when it hit him—this is how Emily must have felt when he'd left her before—on their first honeymoon.

Gabe pulled into his covered parking space and just sat in the car, staring out across the open common area. The sprinklers had come on and the setting sun made rainbows in the mist.

He'd thought he and Emily were so in tune with each other, that she hadn't needed all the hoopla surrounding the wedding. He'd thought it was mostly Freddie's idea anyway and he hadn't minded because Emily seemed to go along with it.

Now, he realized that she was more than "going along with it." She'd needed the ceremony and the honeymoon to make the transition to married life. Gabe hadn't needed it. Once he'd decided Emily was the woman he wanted to spend the rest of his life with, that was it for him. They'd known each other for several years, but they'd only been married for a few days.

For Emily, it hadn't been enough.

This understanding was what Dr. Weber had sensed he lacked. It looked like all those sessions with her had paid off. He understood now. Big time. He felt frustrated and ineffective and...empty. Incredibly empty.

And Emily had been a new bride after a huge wedding when he'd left her...she'd probably felt worse. God, how could he have been such an idiot? Why had it taken him so long to figure it out?

Maybe he shouldn't have left today, either, except that the circumstances were different.

Today, he'd had no right to stay. Slowly, he got out of the car, avoided the sprinklers and unlocked the door to his sterile apartment. Any of his possessions that weren't going into the biosphere with him had gone into storage already. There was a shoebox of pictures he wished he had right now. He wanted to look at the ones of Emily from when they'd been dating. And their wedding. He wanted to look at their wedding pictures. They were just some photos a friend had taken with one of those disposable cameras. Emily had the formal portrait book. Or he assumed she still had it. Maybe not.

Since he hadn't stopped for anything to eat on the way home, Gabe pulled open the fridge and stared inside. He didn't see anything he liked, so he poured himself a bowl of cereal and milk and ate that.

As he crunched, he thought about Emily, this new Emily. She'd gained an attractive self-assurance that combined with her prettiness made her a compellingly attractive woman. A self-sufficient woman. She'd been a little clingy when they'd been dating.

How had she remained friends with the domineering Freddie and still managed to mature with such poise?

When she talked about her decision to have a child, she didn't mention her friend once, so Gabe figured it had been Emily's idea all the way. It was a fairly radical idea for the shyly traditional Emily to want to raise a child on her own, as well.

He stopped chewing. It might be his child, too.

And she'd wanted him to leave.

Gabe stared at the cereal, no longer hungry. They'd had something going between them. He couldn't have been wrong about that. It wasn't all just about making a baby. He still loved her and she must still love him.

Didn't she?

There are legal issues, as well.

I'll sign anything you want.

Gabe held his head in his hands. What had he done?

Late the next afternoon, Gabe called Emily without knowing what he was going to say, just knowing that he had to hear her voice.

She was in a meeting. He didn't leave a message.

He called the next morning.

She was in a meeting. He didn't leave a message.

He called her at home, but she didn't answer. He didn't leave a message.

He called her an hour later and this time left a message. "Hi, Em, this is Gabe. I was just checking to see how you were doing." He let a few seconds pass then said, "Call me if you need anything," and left his number.

She didn't call.

Emily was so busy trying to get the legal framework prepared for the biosphere toy project in time for EduPlaytion to show the prototypes to the press on the day the biospheres were sealed, that she didn't have time to think about Gabe—more than once or twice an hour.

She was proud of herself for sending him away. It had been hideously difficult, but it was for the best. It hurt now, but it would have been unbearable later. She'd found herself enjoying the memories of the weekend a little too much. Wanting a little more.

To counter them, she'd immersed herself in work and barely noticed the passing of the days.

Late one night when she dragged herself home, she found that he'd left a message on her answering machine. "Call if you need anything."

"I need a husband and a father for my child," Emily said to the machine. "Are you ready to be that? No." She erased the message.

Gabe didn't call again.

Nearly two weeks later, the day before the teams were scheduled to enter the biospheres, Emily bought two different pregnancy tests and brought them home.

She didn't feel any different, physically, but these tests claimed to be the most sensitive on the market and she couldn't stand not knowing a moment longer, couldn't stand not knowing before Gabe entered the biosphere in case he might change his mind.

No. She couldn't think that way.

Following the instructions for each test, Emily left them in her bathroom and nervously went into the kitchen to make herself a salad for dinner.

It was far too hot to cook. Besides, she was too excited to eat.

This could be it. Her long-held dream might have taken a big step toward becoming a reality.

Emily looked at her watch and the clock on the oven. There were two minutes difference between them, but still, it was almost time to check the tests. She made herself take a sip of water, then headed for her bathroom.

The knock on her door stopped her and she veered into the foyer to answer it. It had better not be the neighbor kids about their basketball again. When she didn't have any plants in her backyard, it hadn't mattered that the ball came bouncing over the fence so often, but the last couple of times, she'd been left with broken flowers.

She pulled open the door, remembering the last time she thought it had been the kids about their basketball and it had been—

Gabe.

*   *   *

As the days passed, Gabe found himself thinking about Emily. Did she regret their weekend together? Was she pregnant? Surely she'd tell him. There were those legal papers she mentioned, as well. If she were pregnant, she'd want him to sign them.

But as the day he had to fly to Arizona with his team grew closer and Gabe still hadn't heard from Emily, he became annoyed.

She could have at least returned his calls—or the one she knew about. What was he going to have to do, have his secretary call hers and schedule an appointment?

Maybe if he *did* approach this as Nutritional Engineering to EduPlaytion he'd get her attention. He'd certainly get somebody's.

No, he couldn't do that to her. And so he waited. And waited.

On the day before he was scheduled to fly out, Gabe drove to Emily's house. He wanted to say goodbye and he wanted to say it in person. In private. And maybe for a long time.

Then she opened the door and everything he'd planned to say went out of his head.

She was wearing shorts and a sleeveless white blouse. Her feet were bare and she looked great. So great, that Gabe wanted to scoop her off the threshold and cart her off to the bedroom. He had a feeling that wouldn't go over well.

Emily hadn't moved from the doorway. She was regarding him warily, as though he were a stranger selling something door-to-door. As though their weekend together had never happened.

"Hello, Em," he said. "May I come in?" From the expression on her face, he figured he had about a fifty-fifty chance.

With obvious reluctance, Emily stepped away from her front door so that he could enter.

She hadn't said anything and the silence between them was strained and awkward.

Gabe had no idea what he could say to smooth things between them, but he knew for certain that he couldn't blurt out a question about whether or not she was pregnant yet. Besides, she would have told him, wouldn't she?

He walked over to the sofa, wondered if he should sit there, then decided avoiding it would look worse.

Emily, arms wrapped around herself, still stood by the door.

"How have you been?"

"Fine," she answered.

They looked at each other.

"I'm flying to Arizona tomorrow morning," he said finally.

Emily nodded tightly and advanced toward the couch, carefully sitting on a matching overstuffed chair next to it. "We've been preparing to introduce the toys during the press conference."

It was his turn to nod. They both knew these things, but at least they were talking.

"How are the toys coming along?" *I don't care about the toys. I care about you.*

"We have seed envelopes and soil packets, along with plastic biospheres that kids can use on their own. And, the Science Commission is coordinating an effort to donate larger biospheres to selected high schools so science classes can replicate the experiments next fall. Dr. Marta Elkins is going to be the biosphere contact. When she plants her crop, the schools will plant theirs and compare results.'' She was beginning to sound like him.

''I'd heard something about that. Marta staked out a spot by the radishes. Which is fine by me. I don't particularly like radishes anyway.''

Emily smiled. ''I remember.''

She'd smiled. Gabe relaxed marginally. ''Anyway, I did want to see you before I left.''

Her smile faded and Gabe's ease faded with it.

''Why?'' she asked.

Trust Gabe to show up at all the most significant moments of her life.

They'd already said their goodbyes, so why had he come here?

Emily concentrated on detaching her emotions from the situation and giving Gabe her courtroom face. Detaching had always been difficult for her and Freddie had practiced with her over and over.

It hadn't all been one-way, though. Freddie had tunnel vision and Emily had been able to help her learn to step aside and come at a problem from a different angle.

She wished she had Freddie's tunnel vision right now. *I'm a lawyer and Gabe is a client. Concentrate on that.*

''I did want to see you before I left,'' he said.

''Why?'' she asked.

"Emily!" Was that hurt in his eyes? "I wanted to see you," he repeated. "To say goodbye, I guess."

"We already said goodbye."

A muscle jumped in his jaw. He was gritting his teeth. "Also, you, ah, mentioned legal papers?"

Legal papers. The papers that would terminate his parental rights.

Any hope that he might have changed his mind during the past two weeks died within Emily. Their weekend had meant as little to him as their marriage. Whether or not she was pregnant, he still planned to enter the biosphere.

"Do I need to sign any papers?" he persisted.

"In other words, you want to know if I'm pregnant or not," she said, bringing the topic right out in the open.

He drew a deep breath. "*Do* you know if you're pregnant or not?"

Emily was a lawyer. The outcome of entire cases could hinge on the way questions were worded to a witness. "No, I don't know," she could answer truthfully.

There was another awkward silence. Though she despised herself for it, Emily desperately wanted Gabe to tell her that if she were pregnant, he wouldn't go into the biosphere—that he'd stay and they'd raise their child together.

How could he walk away from his own child?

How could she love someone who'd walk away from his own child?

But on the other hand, if a child were the only

reason he'd stay with her, then she didn't want him to. He had to want the whole package and she was part of that package.

"When will you know?" Gabe asked.

"Soon."

"And then?"

"And then, if all goes well, nine months later I'll have a baby."

"I know that."

"Then what do you want me to say?"

He wanted her to ask him to stay, Gabe realized. He wanted her to say, "If I'm having your child, I want you to be there."

But she didn't.

Gabe stared at her carefully impassive face and numbly realized that Emily didn't care if he went into the biosphere, or not. She truly only thought of him as a donor for her child.

And Gabe realized that he desperately hoped she *was* carrying his child. "You'll let me know?" He stood.

Emily stood, as well. "If there's anything you should know."

Gabe supposed he was going to have to be satisfied with that. "Goodbye, Em."

She followed him to the door. He reached for the knob and stopped, turned and reached for Emily instead.

He gazed at her, his eyes tracing the contours of her face, memorizing her features, then he kissed her once, hard, and strode through the door, down the walk and out of her life.

She'd held up just fine until he kissed her. And the way he'd looked at her. If he'd kissed her that way ten years ago, she never would have let him get on that plane by himself.

Emily closed the door and blinked back tears, then she started walking toward the bathroom, her steps getting faster and faster until she was running.

Once there, with her lips still warm from Gabe's goodbye kiss, Emily learned that she was going to have his child.

She walked toward the counter and stared at a Plus sign on one test and all the appropriate stripes on the other.

A baby. She was going to have a baby! She was really pregnant.

There couldn't be a mistake—not with two different tests.

A baby! Emily put her hands over her still-flat stomach. She didn't feel any different, and she didn't have any of the symptoms described in the pregnancy books she'd read. But it was still very early yet.

She was going to have a baby!

Gabe's baby. Emily caught her breath, then ran to the front window and looked out. She had to tell him.

His car was gone and she felt a sharp pang of disappointment before she realized that it was best that he wasn't here.

No, she'd be so excited and happy and emotional and he would have said something like, "That's great, Em." And then he would have gone into the stupid biosphere anyway instead of helping her pick colors for the nursery and names for the baby and coming with her to childbirth classes.

No, she was going to have to do all that alone, just as she'd planned. Sure, Freddie would be there for her, but when it came time to go home at night, Freddie would have Hunter and Emily would have memories.

It was all up to her, now. She'd known it was going to be difficult and that she was going to have to get used to doing things by herself. A lot of things.

But that didn't mean she couldn't be happy. That didn't mean she couldn't start picking out wallpaper and officially decorate the nursery.

And that didn't mean she couldn't call Freddie.

Emily grabbed the phone from the kitchen and brought it into the living room and sat on the sofa, burrowing into the cushions. She'd been avoiding it, treating it as though it was some sort of shrine, which was just silly.

Gabe was out of her life. Gone.

And she liked her sofa, so she was going to sit on it.

Quickly punching out Freddie's number, she just as quickly disconnected.

Wait a minute. Just how much was she prepared to tell Freddie? Did she want her friend knowing that Gabe was the father? Why or why not?

And knowing Freddie, she'd want to know all the details. Emily wanted to keep the details to herself. But then Freddie would wonder why, since she would assume that Emily had gone the donor route.

Would it be bad for Freddie to know Gabe was the father? Would she keep the secret? *Could* she?

Emily returned the phone to the kitchen. This was going to take some thought and she might as well start anticipating questions and the answers she wanted to give before she started announcing her pregnancy.

And she probably ought to make a doctor's appointment, first, as well, just to make sure.

Reaching into the kitchen drawer, Emily got out paper and pen, then carried her salad over to the table and started making a list of questions and answers while she ate.

The biggest question was when was she going to tell Gabe?

Or should she?

Emily flipped the paper over and drew a line down the center of the page. On one side she wrote Tell, and on the other Don't tell.

She'd have to tell him eventually. Even the donors were notified when a live birth occurred. Okay, so the columns became, Tell Now, Tell Later, and Tell After Birth.

Emily stared at the paper and slowly crossed out Tell Now.

Gabe had enough to think about.

The next morning, Emily wore her suit with the slimmest skirt to work, knowing that it would be the first of her regular wardrobe to fall by the wayside.

At noon, everyone at EduPlaytion gathered in the largest conference room and watched the biosphere press conference on television. They were all interested in the toy presentation, but Emily was watching as the three biosphere teams were introduced by satellite hookup. The television network broadcast the three locations at the same time on the screen.

Gabe was already in Arizona. Emily stared at his third of the split screen, trying to see the members of his team. She'd known there were both men and women, but now she had an intense interest in the women he'd be living with for two years.

Her hands went clammy all of a sudden. It had never occurred to her that Gabe might fall in love and marry someone else. She'd always known his work had taken top priority in his life. But what better woman to fall in love with than someone who shared that work?

As Emily watched he smiled his Gabe smile at the press, answered questions, and looked happy and carefree. He'd probably forgotten all about her and their baby, which to be fair, he knew nothing about. But he'd known it was a possibility.

When the camera moved in for a close-up as he was asked a question, Emily saw that beginning-of-the-project look in his eyes, the one that burned with passion for his work.

Once she saw that look on his face, Emily knew she'd made the right choice in not telling him about the baby.

Maybe she wouldn't ever tell him.

Then someone gave a signal and the doors to the three biospheres opened. The crews waved and went inside.

Gabe was the last. When he reached the door, he turned and gave an extra wave looking straight at the camera.

Before she could catch herself, Emily waved back.

And the door closed, sealing the father of her child inside for two years.

CHAPTER EIGHT

THE day after her preliminary visit to the doctor, Emily felt she had to tell somebody about the baby—other than the doctor—or burst.

Freddie was her first and only choice. Emily wasn't quite ready to announce their untraditional impending grandparenthood to her extremely traditional parents and maybe Freddie might have some ideas about how she could tell them. Or when.

Besides the big gala anniversary party had been last weekend and Emily had been waiting to hear from Freddie on how Hunter had responded to Freddie's own desire for a baby. Knowing that she was finally going to achieve her dream of motherhood helped take the sting out of the evening for Emily, and she was able to sincerely congratulate Hunter and Freddie. She hoped the reason she hadn't heard from Freddie was that she and Hunter were already working on a playmate for Emily's baby.

Everything was, at long last, going to be so perfect.

She arrived at their favorite restaurant, It's a Wrap, and when Freddie hadn't arrived after fifteen minutes, she went ahead and ordered a bacon and avocado wrap sandwich, which was what Freddie always ordered.

The order arrived and still no Freddie. Well, if

Freddie stood her up, then Emily would just take the sandwich home with her and have it for dinner.

The thought didn't appeal. In fact, Emily stared at the sandwich on the plate across from her feeling a growing queasiness at the whole idea of eating either bacon or avocado, let alone together.

She swallowed, then swallowed again. She could smell the bacon...and she didn't want to smell bacon. It was making her stomach go all funny.

And then realization struck—morning sickness! She had morning sickness. Or rather noon sickness.

Emily sat very still and promised that if everything already in her stomach would just stay there, she wouldn't add anything to it.

That *would* be the moment Freddie finally arrived.

She looked terrible, but not terrible in a morning-sickness way. Terrible as in she'd forgotten her makeup and had to borrow someone else's who used all the wrong colors.

Emily swallowed carefully, and tried to smile.

"Sorry I'm late. Oh, good, you ordered." Freddie dumped her purse and a shopping bag in the booth and slid across the seat. After a long drink of iced tea, she bit into the sandwich.

Emily closed her eyes and swallowed again. "Freddie, where were you—at a cosmetic counter freebie makeover?"

Freddie eyed her warily over her sandwich. Emily wished she'd put it down. "Why?"

"Well, your makeup looks...weird."

Freddie dug in her purse for a compact mirror. "It doesn't look sexy and alluring?"

"No," Emily told her with the freedom only a long-standing friend could get away with.

But Freddie's reaction was astounding. Tears welled in her eyes. "But I need to look sexy and alluring!"

"Unless that's waterproof mascara you're wearing, you're in trouble."

Freddie dabbed at her eyes. It was not waterproof. "By the way, you could use some of this blush. You're looking positively green."

"Never mind that. What's going on?"

Freddie bit her bright red lip. "I think Hunter is having an affair."

Emily forgot all about her queasy stomach. "No! Not Hunter. I don't believe it. It's just not his style."

"H-he doesn't want a baby!"

"Yes, he does—he's been after you for years to have a baby!"

"Not anymore."

Freddie broke down and told Emily about a terrible scene after her anniversary party when Hunter told her he didn't think it was right to bring children into a marriage where the parents barely knew each other.

Emily uneasily wondered what Hunter's opinion would be of what she and Gabe had done.

As she listened to Freddie detail what sounded like a complete marital breakdown, she wanted to be sympathetic, but couldn't help selfishly wondering how she would be affected. Having Hunter as a father figure to her child had been an important part of her overall plan. What would happen if Freddie and Hunter's marriage broke apart?

Emily was immediately ashamed of herself. She *was* being selfish. Freddie was suffering a pain Emily knew all too well and she should be thinking of her friend's feelings. "What are you going to do?"

"I've been following him," Freddie confessed in a small voice.

"Oh, Freddie. How pathetic."

"No. I'm trying to get to know him. He said we didn't know each other…only he's not trying to get to know me, he's trying to get to know somebody else! And she's—she's blonde!"

The tears welled up again and Freddie wasn't a crier. "But I am going to get him back, I swear. And I want you to help me."

"Sure, anything," Emily rashly promised.

"Thanks." Freddie gripped her hand. "You're a good friend and I didn't mean to dump all this on you." She sniffed. "But I thought I ought to tell you because 'Project Pregnancy' is going to have to wait— that is if you're still interested in having our babies at the same time."

Emily just sat there.

"I'm sorry, Em. I know how gung ho you were with the donor idea, but it shouldn't be…" Freddie trailed off and narrowed her mascara-smudged eyes at Emily. "Shouldn't be too much longer."

Emily swallowed.

"You aren't eating your lunch," Freddie commented and inched Emily's plate closer to her.

Emily moved back an inch. "You just told me you thought your husband is having an affair and you expect me to chomp lettuce through it?"

"I'm finished with the bad news. You can eat now."

"Well, okay, I will." Emily stared down at the Mediterranean grilled veggie wrap she'd ordered. The vinegar from the marinade seemed particularly strong today.

She picked up the sandwich, then abruptly set it down again. "Maybe in a minute. I'm still upset for you." Glancing across the table, she found herself being scrutinized by Fredericka Welles Loren Cole, attorney.

"You're pregnant, aren't you?"

Emily gasped. "How can you tell?"

"When you're upset, you eat," Freddie said. "When you're happy, you eat. When you're on a diet, you eat. You're not eating, so you're obviously pregnant."

Which was why Freddie was one of the best attorneys in Houston.

"Aren't you?"

She shouldn't feel so happy when Freddie was so miserable, but Emily nodded, unable to suppress a smile as she did so.

"Oh, Em!" Freddie's face softened. "I'm so h-happy for *youuuuuu!*" And she sobbed quietly into her napkin.

"Freddie, things will work out for you, too." But maybe not the way she wanted them to.

Freddie wiped her eyes, pretty much removing the

last of the mascara. "Not if I keep blubbering like this. Can you imagine if this happens when I'm in court?"

"Not a chance."

Freddie gave her a weak grin. "Hey, I'm truly happy for you. Gee, it went quick, didn't it? We were just looking at possible donors a few weeks ago. In fact, I thought you had to interview with doctors and have a check up and fill out forms...and chart your temperature... It sounded like a several-month process," Freddie said thoughtfully.

Emily's heart sank as Freddie turned lawyer on her. "I've been charting my temperature."

"I see. So which donor did you pick? Not the bodybuilder."

"No. Not the bodybuilder."

Freddie stared at her, waiting.

Emily stared back, but she'd never been as good at staring as Freddie.

"Did he have curly brown hair and dark eyes?" Freddie asked softly.

"Yes," Emily whispered.

Freddie blinked and Emily felt her cheeks grow warm.

"Oh, Emily...does he know?"

She shook her head.

"You've got to tell him."

It was Emily's turn to get weepy. "Why?"

"You know why."

"No, I don't. It's *my* baby. He doesn't care—he's in that stupid biosphere!"

"Maybe he wouldn't be in that stupid biosphere if he knew you were going to have his baby!"

"And do you think I want him on those terms?"

"Yeah," Freddie said. "I do."

Everything was perfect. Gabe stood in the exact center of the desert biosphere and looked all around him. With this project, he'd achieved everything he'd ever wanted and on a scale he'd only dared imagine in his dreams.

He was in charge and the experiments were being conducted just the way he wanted them to be. There was a huge public awareness about the challenge of providing enough food for the growing population and a new nutrient-dense combo of soy and kale was proving almost impossible to kill in all three biospheres.

This was it. The pinnacle of his career.

But instead of enjoying himself, he desperately wondered if Emily was pregnant. It had been exactly a month since their weekend. She should know by now. She would have told him, wouldn't she?

Wouldn't she?

"…and at about seven months, you can sign up for childbirth classes. Do you have someone who can be your coach?" the doctor asked Emily.

It was her second visit. "Yes, my friend Freddie."

"Oh, good. Well, tell him that he's welcome to come with you on your prenatal visits—"

"Freddie is a woman. Fredericka."

The doctor didn't miss a beat. "She's welcome as well."

Emily left the doctor's office armed with booklets and instructions and vitamin prescriptions and the intense feeling that she'd made a huge mistake.

Being pregnant with Gabe's child wasn't the solace she'd expected. She missed him. She wanted to share all this with him.

She'd heard the baby's heartbeat today, a fast whooshing sound that made everything real to her. She and the nurse had smiled at each other in that incredibly wondrous moment and Emily desperately wished Gabe could have been there, too.

There were going to be a lot of these moments, and it was only going to get worse after the baby was born. Every time she looked at his child, she was going to be reminded of Gabe and her hopeless love. Why hadn't she anticipated this? What was the matter with her? Had she really thought that she could just have Gabe's baby without having Gabe, too?

"And so we're all agreed?" Marta Elkins asked.

It was the weekly conference and Gabe's entire team was seated around the polished wooden table in a lushly shaded part of the biosphere. They might have been having a picnic, but they definitely weren't.

These conferences were supposed to provide a forum for unemotional complaints and suggestions. Dr. Weber had suggested them, and Gabe had gone along, but right now, they were just time wasters, as far as he was concerned. When the team had been here long enough to have real problems, then these sessions would be valuable.

They'd been in the biosphere for three weeks. Emily had to know if she was pregnant by now. He could hardly stand not knowing. He was checking his e-mail and telephone messages three times a day, for pity's sake.

Was everything all right with her? How did she feel? And if she weren't pregnant, how was she handling the disappointment?

"Gabe?" Marta arched an eyebrow at him.

He didn't know if he could take two years of her arched eyebrows. "Great," he said. "Sounds fine."

They all exchanged looks.

"What?"

"You haven't been paying attention."

"Sure I have. We were discussing altering humidity levels to more closely mimic the desert."

"We voted on that ten minutes ago. We've been discussing battery acid disposal." Marta gazed impassively at him. "You just agreed to dump it on the plants in the southwest quadrant."

"Did I?"

Marta gave him a wintry smile.

"Then I apologize." Gabe didn't like Marta. With that Ph.d. after her name, she thought she was superior to him. She completely discounted the fact that he had years more field experience than she did. He didn't have the degree, so he couldn't possibly be the expert he claimed to be.

Right. And how did this one slip by Dr. Weber?

Gabe was going to have to confront Marta before things got out of hand. He couldn't have his authority challenged like this.

On the other hand, he *hadn't* been paying attention.

He couldn't concentrate on his work. There had been hours at a stretch when he hadn't thought of his work at all. When was the last time that had happened?

Had it ever?

It was this business with Emily. He couldn't stand not knowing.

As soon as the meeting broke up, Gabe headed for his private quarters and opened his laptop. He was going to have to e-mail Emily and it was going to be tricky. All communication to and from the biosphere was monitored. Letters were supposed to be private, but Gabe guessed that they passed through a censor, as well. There was just too much riding on this project to chance any industrial spying or data leaks before the sponsors had first crack at the information.

How to word his e-mail to maintain their privacy? He didn't know how Emily wanted to handle any announcements. It took Gabe a full thirty minutes to carefully craft a message to her. It was a little cryptic, but he figured she'd understand because there was a disclaimer at the bottom of all outgoing and incoming communication warning that it was monitored.

Now all he had to do was wait for an answer.

* * *

She sure felt pregnant now. Emily, never a napper, wanted to curl up in the afternoons and for the past week had fallen asleep right after she got home from work, waking in the middle of the night. Then it was hard to go back to sleep.

Okay, if this was the crazy schedule her body wanted, then she wasn't going to argue. Like she had a chance of winning, anyway.

And so, at 3:00 a.m., she got up, made herself a cup of hot strawberry milk—milk in which she stirred a spoon of strawberry jelly—which was about the only thing that didn't upset her stomach, and opened her laptop. She'd learned to work when she felt like it so when she didn't, she wouldn't fall so far behind.

Emily scanned her list of incoming e-mail and stopped when she saw one with the return address of *GV@AZbiosphere.com.*

Gabe.

Emily clicked on it first and stared at the single word.

Well?

Well? *Well?* How dare he! She had heard nothing from him for weeks and he can only spare her a single word? Angrily, she typed back, "Well, what?"

On Thursday, Gabe did the unthinkable: he made a mistake. It was a serious one, but not a large one. Just a warning mistake. Just a pay-attention-and-stop-thinking-about-Emily alert.

There had been no answering e-mail from her and

he'd been thinking about what that meant, when he watered the wrong row of delta3rv2 verdigrum carrots before he realized what he was doing. These carrots weren't supposed to get water. The control carrots were. Now he'd ruined this cycle's experiment for this particular strain.

The carrots tasted like alfalfa anyway. They may be full of nutrients, but who could get past the taste?

He slumped onto one of the plastic stools that were scattered throughout the area. Maybe he could salvage something from the planting. Say, the effects of heavy watering twice early in the growth cycle. Maybe extra water would improve the taste.

Right. He could imagine Marta's face when he made that suggestion.

He wished he could see Emily's.

He couldn't stand it. Leaving everything, he walked back to his quarters and turned on his computer, closing his eyes in relief when he saw the message from Emily.

Well, what? He blinked. That was all? Had she written more and the censors deleted it, or was that all she'd written?

If the computer program had detected any key words to flag the contents of the mail, he would have had a message to that effect. There was no message.

Was she toying with him? Teasing him? Punishing him?

How was he supposed to know without seeing her or hearing her voice inflections? Telephone calls were discouraged, and very definitely monitored.

"Did you pass your test?" he typed back.

*   *   *

Emily wasn't at all surprised to find the additional message from Gabe the next time she checked her mail. But how to answer?

She knew good and well what he was asking, and since he'd spaced his message near the bottom just above a sentence that read, *Warning: All communication may be monitored by a third party for security purposes* she at last figured out the reason for his brevity.

Still. Still he could have typed a *little* more. But he obviously didn't want to take more than a few seconds away from his precious work. She was surprised he'd bothered to ask at all.

Emily sat back in her desk chair, hands lightly skimming over her stomach. If seeing Gabe again was a test, then she'd failed. Miserably.

She'd allowed herself to become emotionally involved when she'd known it would only lead to heartbreak. She'd tried to emotionally detach herself from him and the first time her resolve was tested, look what had happened.

"No," she typed back and pushed Send before she could change her mind.

She'd tell him about the baby someday when her recent heart wounds had healed. Besides, what difference would it make to him to know now? He'd still be in the biosphere and she'd still be raising their child alone.

This way, he wouldn't contact her anymore and the healing could begin.

* * *

Gabe didn't know how long he sat in his private quarters and stared at that one word.

No.

So final, that "no." During the past weeks he'd been thinking—too much—of possibilities, of what having a baby with Emily would be like. Of being with Emily again. Of raising their child together. The baby would be their link—forever. Something that was part Gabe and part Emily.

And with one word, she'd destroyed all hope he had of getting back into her life.

Was Emily relieved, or disappointed? Wouldn't she have rather had his child than some stranger's?

Gabe honestly didn't know anymore.

At last, his dark room lit only by the computer screen, he typed, "I'm sorry, Em." And he was—sorry for her and sorry for himself.

Sorry for what might have been.

Couldn't he have at least asked what her plans were? Added something? Told her a little about life in the biosphere? Asked her about the toys? Anything?

Emily couldn't believe she raced through the traffic to get home and check her e-mail for that. She'd logged on twice from the office, though she didn't like getting her personal e-mail there, and there hadn't been anything. Gabe's messages seemed to come through in the evening. Emily imagined him eating dinner and then going to his room, or wherever he lived in the biosphere, and writing to her.

She was so pitiful. His entire communication with

her had consisted of less than a dozen words, yet here she was, hoping for more.

Say he had written more. What would it matter? If she *had* told him she was pregnant, would anything have changed? No. Gabe would still be the same Gabe who was more interested in his work than committing to a family.

It was better that she didn't respond.

Gabe checked his watch. There hadn't been a message from Emily yesterday morning, or evening, or this morning, either. So maybe she didn't check her mail every day.

Maybe she was devastated by not being pregnant.

Or maybe she wasn't going to respond.

When the third day passed without a response from her, Gabe realized she wasn't going to write. She wanted nothing to do with him.

The least he could do was respect her wishes.

"Have you told him yet?" Freddie asked with her usual bluntness.

"No."

Emily and Freddie were making their first foray into a maternity clothing shop. Emily wouldn't need maternity clothes for weeks, but they wanted to check out the styles.

"Oh, my gosh, that's horrible!" Freddie said.

"No, it isn't. I *will* tell him, but why bother now? What could he do about it?"

"I wasn't talking about telling Gabe, but the fact that you haven't is horrible, too. I was referring to that awful flowered thing you're holding. What is *with* that collar? And the giant sleeves? Do they think women get pregnant in their arms?''

Emily put the dress back on the rack. It *was* pretty awful.

''Can't you just see me in a courtroom wearing one of those things?'' Freddie grimaced. ''I'd lose all credibility with the jury.''

Emily laughed. ''You might get more sympathy that way.''

''You, know, Em, I'm seeing a great business opportunity here.''

''Freddie, we're just in a mall. I'm sure they have businesswomen type maternity clothing somewhere. Although...'' Emily held up a navy blue T-shirt with the words Under Construction and an arrow pointing downward on it.

''No,'' Freddie said firmly.

''I suppose you'll veto the ducks, as well.''

''Emily, would you buy anything with ducks on it if you *weren't* pregnant?''

''No.''

''So when are you going to tell him?'' Freddie was relentless and tricky. Her favorite tactic was to change the subject, then throw in a question just when a person had relaxed.

She got a lot of answers that way. It didn't work this time because Emily didn't have an answer to give her.

Every morning and night for a week, she'd been checking her e-mail, and there hadn't been any further communication from Gabe. He was obviously only interested in whether or not she was pregnant, and now, though she didn't exactly lie to him, she knew he believed that she wasn't, and guess what? He'd expressed no more interest in her whatsoever.

What a surprise.

It looked like she wasn't the only one who'd failed a test.

Fall in the desert meant a break in the heat.

The cooling system in the living quarters of the biosphere hadn't been able to keep up with the heat, which had been greater inside than had been calculated by the engineers.

The entire team had been cranky. After endless meetings, they'd decided to switch some of their experiments to nighttime when it was considerably cooler. It would be more practical for farmers then as well.

For some reason, working alone at night made Gabe think of Emily. He thought about her a lot, and though to the others, he was a good worker, Gabe knew his efficiency had dropped.

He wanted to see her. And since he couldn't go to her, that meant he had to figure out a way to get her to come to him.

He sat in front of his computer and typed any number of beginnings to e-mails.

"Hi, Emily. How are things with you? We're all fine here."

He sounded like a fourth-grader writing home from camp.

"Hi, Emily. I've read the official progress reports

with the toy tie-in, but I was wondering what your private take on it was?"

That didn't work, either.

"Hi, Emily. How have you been? We've found a strain of wheat that'll grow if somebody forty miles away spits in the wind."

Perhaps not.

While Gabe was sitting there, an e-mail came through from Larry, the Nutritional Engineering president.

Gabe, We need your okay on the final contracts for the experiments the schools are doing with Marta. They'll need to get started by the second week in September so they can finish by Christmas break. Shall I let the lawyers okay the toys for you?

Of course the lawyers could okay the toys for him. That's what he paid them for. Gabe started to reply, then stopped.

Smiling to himself, he typed, "Larry: I want to see the products before they're sent to the schools. It's time we all had another face-to-face powwow anyway. Obviously, I can't come to you, so get with the EduPlaytion people and their lawyers, and bring everybody out here for a meeting."

CHAPTER NINE

IF EMILY had to see Gabe, then this was the ideal time. The end of summer brought the end of her morning sickness and she was still wearing most of her regular clothes. And since she'd be wearing a suit jacket, Gabe would never know she was pregnant.

They saw the biosphere gleaming in the desert sun long before they reached it in the van they'd rented. With Emily was her assistant, a couple of NASA people and the EduPlaytion development team. The Nutritional Engineering president was also supposed to be there, but had gone ahead to make preparations.

They would have to go through decontamination procedures and any papers they brought into the biosphere would have to as well. Still, as Emily understood it, Gabe would be behind a glass screen.

Honestly, she knew they wanted to keep the atmosphere contained, but the whole procedure seemed like a trip into outer space.

They had to shower. Emily couldn't believe it. They weren't even going to come into contact with Gabe and his precious plants.

And, true, Emily was miffed because her careful makeup and hairstyle was ruined. When they had to put on these white jumpsuits, she realized she could have been ready to deliver the baby and Gabe wouldn't have known it.

She made do with slicking her damp hair back into a ponytail and using the lipstick and mascara she'd brought—after they'd been irradiated, for pity's sake—but knew she hadn't achieved the devastatingly attractive look-what-you-gave-up effect she'd wanted.

He was waiting for them when they trooped into the makeshift conference room.

They stared at each other through the glass.

Well, *he* looked good.

He was more tanned than he'd been. Emily knew being tanned wasn't good for you, but did it have to look so darn attractive?

And how did a person get tanned in a biosphere, anyway?

Without thinking, Emily took the seat directly opposite Gabe and continued to drink in the sight of him after four months.

He gave her a tentative smile that went straight to her heart.

She smiled back. How could she help it? She loved him and realized that hopeless, or not, she always would.

Someone cleared his throat and Emily was suddenly aware of her surroundings. Of the other men in the room.

Had they noticed her staring at Gabe like a lovestruck teenager looking at her favorite movie star?

Without meeting anyone else's eyes, Emily ripped

open the plastic packet that her papers had been sealed in.

He was in love with her. Still and always.

It had cost a fortune to bring them all out here and put them through decontamination. Larry had been whining about the cost all morning.

Gabe didn't care. It had been worth every penny to see Emily again, or to see her face. He smiled at the sight of her in the bulky white jumpsuit.

And her hair, damp and slicked back, reminded him of the way she looked right after they'd showered together.

Reminded him of the way he'd *felt* after they'd showered together.

He reached for the glass of filtered water and his hands shook with the effort of not leaving the sterile room, jerking open the outside door, and compromising the entire desert biosphere project just for the opportunity to take her in his arms again.

Instead, he looked at the plastic spheres that would be sent to the schools, and flipped through the contracts, pretending to read them. They could be sticking him with a million-dollar bill and he'd sign the contracts anyway.

The sound system gave her voice an electronic quality, and the glass partition was between them, but this was as close to Emily as he'd been in months.

And it wasn't enough.

*   *   *

It was fortunate that Emily had gone over the contracts with the proverbial fine-toothed comb, because she was incapable of absorbing any further information.

Gabe, the father of her baby, was just a few feet away. He might as well be on the moon.

Emily kept sneaking peeks at him as each person present gave a mini-progress report. When it was Gabe's turn, Emily relaxed and allowed herself to stare at him all she wanted.

It was the first time she'd relaxed since she'd walked into the room.

''Dr. Elkins and I think the shorter hybrid of corn would be more appropriate for the class biospheres. It only grows about this high.'' Gabe stood to indicate the height with his hand.

He was wearing khaki shorts. Gabe looked good in shorts.

Emily sighed softly and then she felt it: the tiniest fluttering on one side of her stomach.

She pressed her hand against the area and when she removed it, she felt the sensation again. It was almost a tickle, but not quite.

All at once, Emily knew what it was. The baby! She'd felt the baby move for the first time.

She held herself very still and stared straight at Gabe, her eyes blinking back happy tears as she waited for the feeling to come again. Most of all, she desperately wanted to be able to take his hand and place it on her stomach so he could feel the baby, too.

But she couldn't. Even if he knew about the baby,

she couldn't, not with these infuriating sterile precautions they had to take.

What if she had to bring the baby here? All she could ever do was hold it up to the glass. Gabe would never be able to hold his own child, at least not until the child was fifteen months old and a toddler.

Imagine having a child you couldn't touch. Emily couldn't do that to him.

Right then and there, she vowed to be here with their child on the day Gabe came out of the biosphere, the day when he could hold their child for the first time.

At last the meeting was over. "Okay, I don't know about the rest of you, but I'm ready for a break," Larry announced.

Emily was more than ready for a break. She was starving and was going to have to eat something soon.

"We have box lunches for you all. After you eat, you're welcome to walk the public observation paths and view some of the experiments in biosphere, but once you leave this room, you can't return without going through the decontamination procedures all over again."

Everyone groaned.

Emily practically inhaled her lunch—a salad made of greens and baby vegetables grown in the biosphere, and bread made from wheat grown here as well.

Gabe didn't eat with them and she was afraid she

wasn't going to be able to see him again, when he returned and gestured to her.

She walked over to the glass. "I've got a few questions—if you're willing to stay a little longer."

"Jack can probably answer them," Larry offered helpfully.

Gabe said nothing, but the look he gave his company president almost shouted "go away!"

"On the other hand, perhaps it's better that you get your questions answered from the source." Larry looked around. "Anybody up for the grand tour?"

Gabe flipped through the contracts until the others had left.

"What questions did you have?" Emily asked.

He smiled. "How have you been?" he asked softly, or as softly as the sound system would let him.

I just felt your child move inside me.

It was so hard not to tell him everything and to share the wonder of the growing life inside her.

But she didn't dare. It would be hard enough to walk away in an hour or so. She couldn't keep putting herself through these emotional upheavals. It couldn't be good for the baby and it sure wasn't good for her.

"I've been fine," she answered. "Work is keeping me busy. A children's television show wants to do a feature and we had to race to produce toys for it."

"I know." He smiled and his eyes traced the contours of her face. "They filmed out here a couple of weeks ago. Cute kids.''

Emily nodded.

Gabe looked around the room, smiled apologetically and asked, ''Have you…?'' He finished with a gesture.

''No,'' Emily said quickly. She knew he was asking if she'd chosen a donor yet.

''Oh.''

''As I said, work keeps me busy. You know how that goes.''

''Yeah.'' He didn't smile.

They were silent for a minute. ''About the contracts,'' Emily began.

''They're fine,'' Gabe told her. ''I just wanted the chance to talk with you privately—or as privately as we ever get here.''

As if to illustrate his point, there was a quick knock on Gabe's door and an attractive brunette stuck her head in. ''Gabe, if you're finished here, we've got a leak in the irrigation line in section seventeen.'' She looked dismissively at Emily. ''Probably sending so many people through decontamination at once overloaded the water recycling system.''

Gabe looked at Emily. ''I've got to go.''

She was already gathering her things. ''Of course. Don't you always?''

''Emily—''

''Goodbye, Gabe. See you around.''

Twenty-four hours later, Gabe sat in front of his computer. He was going to e-mail Emily and he was going to keep e-mailing her until he got a response. He wasn't sure what he was going to say, but had he ever been sure what to e-mail her?

It didn't matter. He was after simple contact.

Finally, he just told her about fixing the leak and the plants which would now be joining the ones he'd overwatered. He didn't tell her that he'd overwatered them because he'd been thinking about her and he didn't go into much detail in case the censors got overly enthusiastic with the "delete" key.

He wanted to tell her about Marta Elkins. The woman blamed him for jeopardizing the whole project by asking for the in-person meeting and overloading the biosphere's system resources.

She was probably right. No, there was no "probably" about it. Marta had stopped short of accusing him of calling an unnecessary meeting, but she managed to get her point across.

The meeting may not have been strictly necessary for the project, but it had been absolutely necessary for Gabe. He'd had to see Emily.

And now that he'd seen her, he had to get her back.

...good to see you. Gabe

Emily had read the message four times. If he hadn't signed it, she wouldn't have known it was from Gabe. He'd started out talking about his project and how the leak had ruined one of the experiments. At the first reading, Emily had skimmed through it, wondering why he bothered to tell her.

But then he'd opened up and talked about his disappointment with himself for not considering the delicate balance of the system resources.

Gabe had *never* talked that way to her.

Emily sat in her home office and read his message as she ate strawberry yogurt, finding that a light dinner helped her sleep better.

She felt compelled to respond to him, though she didn't want to. She began by telling him that the school miniature biospheres had been delivered, though he probably already knew. And she also admitted how impressed she was with the scope of the project and his part in it.

"I'm proud of you and proud to be a part of the project, too."

Should she say that to him? To her surprise, she realized it was true. She may resent his devotion to his work, but she was still proud of him.

Sighing, she pressed Send and then turned off her computer and went to bed.

The next evening, she tried to watch the news as she ate her yogurt—blueberry this time—but kept wondering if Gabe had sent her a response.

Finally, she couldn't stand it and turned on her computer. There *was* a message, as long as the other had been. By the time Emily finished reading it, she had tears in her eyes.

It's just that I'm investing two years of my life and I don't want there to be any *mistakes.*

Emily smiled. That sounded very Gabe-like.

You know, Em, about two years ago, I went back to the place where the Sahara project had been.

There had been this kid, Rahim, who would hang around and do errands and chores for us. You should have seen him. His legs were thinner than I thought a human being's legs could get. And his stomach was huge. But once we started feeding him, he grew and his body bulked up. By the time we left, he looked like a normal high-schooler. I thought he was about twelve, but it turned out he was seventeen. When I went back, I asked about him and they said he was gone. I thought they meant that he'd died, but he'd gone away to school. He's going to be a doctor, Em. He's studying in London and he'll come back to practice in the village. Think of it. He was starving to death and now he's going to be a doctor. Food made all the difference.

Emily didn't want to know about the dramatic changes in the village and the crops they were able to grow. That was the place that had destroyed her marriage.

That's why I work so hard, I guess.

Emily didn't want to understand, much less empathize. She didn't want to learn more about the man she'd married so long ago.

She didn't want to fall deeper in love with him.

So she didn't write him back.

After struggling to fall asleep for two hours, Emily flipped on the light. "Oh, all right!"

Shoving her feet into her house shoes, she stormed into her office and angrily typed a message.

"I think it's wonderful to make a difference in someone's life. I wish I'd made a difference in yours."

As soon as she hit Send, she knew it was a mistake and there was no way to retrieve the message.

She sat back in the chair and stared at the screen. When the now-familiar flutters began, she smiled and put her hands on her gently rounded stomach. "Well, kid, your mom just made one doozy of a mistake. The question is, how will your daddy respond?"

Gabe read Emily's message and immediately went to the gym and spent forty-five minutes on the StairMaster.

Emily would never forgive him for leaving her. He'd lost her for good.

By the time he showered and was back in front of his computer, Gabe was actually angry. She was constantly bringing up his mistake. It was long past time to move on. So he typed, "Forgive me?" and sent it.

He typed the same message every day for a week. He'd type it every day for a year, if he had to.

But he didn't. On a Sunday night, fittingly, there was finally a return message from Emily.

OK.

"Have you told him yet?" demanded Freddie, who'd come over to help Emily decorate the nursery. They were hanging wallpaper border.

"No," Emily replied.

"Why not?"

Emily handed a moistened strip to Freddie, who

was on the stepladder. "Because the last three months have been wonderful."

"Wonderful how?"

"Gabe is paying more attention—real attention—to me than he did even when we were engaged."

"So he sends you a couple of e-mails—you call that attention?" Freddie carefully positioned the border.

"He e-mails me every day. We talk about so many things. And he's paying attention to *me* because he wants to, not because I'm carrying his child."

"But you *are* carrying his child."

"He doesn't know that, though."

Freddie smoothed out the wrinkles in the border, then climbed down and moved the stepladder. "I can't believe you went with the ducks."

"They're cute ducks."

"It's a lot of yellow for any kid."

"There's royal blue and white. It's not all yellow." She handed Freddie another strip.

"The royal-blue is the only thing that saves this room from insipidity."

"Is that a word?"

"Yes. I'm serious. If there had been powder-blue in this design, I would not now be giving up my Sunday afternoon."

"Thanks, Freddie."

"So when are you telling him?"

Emily grinned. Freddie's tactics no longer worked. She'd seen that question coming a mile away. "After the baby is born."

"How long after?"

"I don't know. At first, I thought it would be horrible for him to know about the baby and not be able to hold it, but now…" She sighed. "I don't know. Besides, I look forward to Gabe's e-mails. I like the way things are between us now. Once he knows about the baby, everything will change. He'll wonder why I haven't told him earlier and accuse me of punishing him."

"Duh."

"Look, Freddie, I'm not proud of that. He'll be angry and…and I don't want the e-mails to end because he's angry."

Freddie gave her a scornful look. "You should have decorated with chickens instead of ducks."

"But…but what if he says 'Congratulations' and acts like nothing is different?"

"Do you think that's a possibility?"

"Maybe—no." She ran both hands through her hair. "I don't know! I've never felt so miserably illogical in my life!"

"Hormones," Freddie said. "You know, one conversation would clear everything up between you two."

"I know." Emily handed her friend another strip. "But that's one conversation I don't want to have."

Freddie sighed. "I knew I should have knocked your heads together."

Emily was gazing out the office window thinking about what Freddie had said when there was an abrupt knock on her door.

"Emily, have you got a minute?" Without waiting for an answer, Bill Stone, Emily's boss, walked into her office and carefully closed the door behind him.

Emily immediately straightened. This couldn't be good news.

"There's been an interesting development with your project," he began even before he sat in the chair next to her desk.

Emily started to get up so she could sit next to him, but he waved her back to her seat.

"A class action suit is being brought by three toy manufacturers challenging the exclusive agreement we have with Nutritional Engineering."

It *was* bad. "On what grounds?"

"As a part of the government, NASA should have taken bids on the contract."

"But Nutritional Engineering isn't a part of the government and our agreement is with them."

Bill templed his fingers and gazed at the ceiling. "It's been touted as a joint project between government and private industry."

"That's the PR people's problem, then."

"It's our problem—or rather your problem. There will be all sorts of accusations made—they're just fishing, hoping to provoke a response and drum up support in the press. They've already taken a few shots, one of which is that there is some connection between EduPlaytion and Nutritional Engineering and we were shown favoritism."

"Well, we were!"

Bill winced and touched his hand to his ear, then

patted his front pocket. "Hearing aid just buzzed. It does that sometimes. Now what did you say?"

Okay, fine. "I wondered what you'd suggest as a counter strategy."

"There's always the 'woman in a position of power being resented by the old guard male' approach. It's usually an effective smoke screen."

Maybe because it was true, Emily thought, but didn't dare say.

"If they persist in the connection angle, you should call a press conference and say something to the effect of a man in your position wouldn't be questioned, but as a young woman, it has to be assumed that you were dating the boss, or some such nonsense. You know the drill."

Emily smiled weakly.

Bill warmed to his own suggestion. "You know, that's a good plan. In fact, why don't we set up a press conference right now before this innuendo has a chance to get entrenched in the public's mind." He reached for the telephone on the lamp table next to the seating area.

"No."

Bill looked quizzically at her, then smiled. "You look fine." He thought she was worried about her appearance. "In fact being pregnant will get you sympathy right off." He punched a button on the phone.

Emily got up from behind her desk. "No, it won't," she said firmly, and then had the temerity to disconnect his call.

Bill's face turned stern. "I don't think you fully comprehend the seriousness of the lawsuit."

It was the touch of patronization in his voice that got to her. "And I don't think you fully comprehend the entire situation. You know Gabriel Valera, the owner of Nutritional Engineering?"

"Yes, yes," Bill said impatiently, his hand still poised over the telephone.

Emily put both hands on her protruding belly. "This is his child."

Bill didn't even blink. After a couple of seconds, he tapped at his ear, then took off his hearing aid. "The battery's gone. It does that sometimes. I believe I'll go get another one."

He strode quickly from the room.

They both knew he'd heard her. In fact rumor was that he didn't need a hearing aid at all.

So she was on her own with this one. Emily stood in her office and wondered if she'd still have a job in the morning. Spreading her fingers over her stomach, she rubbed it lightly. The baby had chosen this moment to turn somersaults.

The baby, she had to think of the baby. She needed her job and the medical benefits. Emily drew a deep breath, as deeply as she could these days, and went back to her desk. If she wanted to keep her job, then she was going to have to come up with another strategy to counter the claims made by the jealous toy companies.

She'd been working furiously for over an hour when a grave-looking Bill came back into her office.

"New battery in the hearing aid, Bill?"

"Yes. Though sometimes a loose connection will cause the thing to go on the blink."

"I understand. I've come up with a strategy to counter the suit."

"Let's hear it." He sat.

"We admit that we got the contract because Gabe and I knew each other from school."

Bill's hand crept toward his ear.

"Your hearing is fine, Bill."

"That's what I was afraid of."

"Oh, it gets worse," Emily said cheerfully. "Gabe and I were married once. I thought I ought to tell you in case some enterprising reporter digs up the connection."

Bill looked like he was going through a bout of morning sickness, himself.

"If we get all defensive, their lawyers will make it look like we have something to be defensive about. So what if we got the contract through personal connections? Men do it all the time."

Bill's gaze dropped to her stomach. "Perhaps not quite so personal."

Emily tilted her chin up. "He doesn't know and I'd like to keep it that way for now."

Drawing a deep breath, Bill leaned back in the chair. "I think it's best if I don't ask who doesn't know what."

"Fair enough. And I've checked our contracts. Our agreement is with Nutritional Engineering only. NASA may have wanted the tie-in, but they're not part of our agreement and they weren't mentioned anywhere in the contracts we have with Nutritional

Engineering. However, they might have a separate agreement with Nutritional Engineering, but that doesn't concern us.''

Bill smiled for the first time since he'd entered the room. "Now that I heard, loud and clear.''

After he left, Emily called a meeting and brainstormed tactics with her team. She was late leaving the office and thinking about getting home to check for Gabe's nightly message when a bright light flooded the sidewalk outside the parking garage.

"Ms. Shaw?''

Another light flashed. "Ms. Shaw, do you have a comment on the suit brought by Hanecker toys?'' A woman thrust a microphone at Emily.

Reporters already? "I'm preparing a statement to release tomorrow.''

"Can you tell our viewers what will be in that statement?''

Viewers? Behind the bright light was a man with a camera propped on his shoulder. It bore the logo of a local television station. They were taping her. Emily moved her briefcase in front of her stomach.

"I'll be happy to tell them tomorrow.'' Emily started walking toward her car. The last thing she wanted was to be on television. If she didn't give them any information, maybe they would go away and leave her alone.

The reporter followed her. "Is there any truth to the allegations of cronyism between your company and Nutritional Engineering?''

"I haven't heard any such allegations, however,

as I have said repeatedly, I am preparing a statement for release tomorrow.''

''If you haven't heard any allegations, then what are you responding to in your statement?''

''Nothing, if you won't let me go home and write it!'' she snapped.

She shouldn't have lost her temper. They were deliberately provoking her and she'd known it, but knowing it hadn't helped. Now, as she got in her car, she heard the reporter talking earnestly into the camera.

Oh, well. Emily supposed she'd find out what the woman said on the ten o'clock news.

CHAPTER TEN

REPORTERS had been hounding Gabe for a statement all day and apparently were prepared to camp out at the biosphere until they got one. Gabe didn't have a statement. He didn't know enough to make a statement.

Larry hadn't been much help and Emily's phone had been busy. Gabe did know that letting the reporters wait in the hot sun was going to result in unflattering stories, so he spoke to them by phone from inside the biosphere and explained that he was currently only involved in the experiments. That didn't satisfy them when they'd traveled all this way for a story, so he had to go into the area of the biosphere that was next to the public walkways and pose for pictures.

He felt like an animal in a cage.

That night, having been alerted about the story by Larry, Gabe and the rest of the biosphere team sat in the recreation room and watched the ten o'clock news.

Film of Gabe looking at plants ran while a commentator recited the allegations in a tone of voice that made him sound like an ax-murderer. They were talking plants and toys here, for pity's sake. Couldn't they focus on the important issues like education and food production?

171

The others were kidding him about his new TV star status when the picture changed and Emily's face flashed on the screen. She'd been ambushed by the press, that was clear, and it was equally clear that she wasn't going to say anything.

Go, Em, he thought.

And then the camera focused on the little blond terrier of a reporter while Emily walked toward her car.

As Gabe stared, a clearly pregnant Emily turned sideways and got into her car.

Emily was pregnant. "Oh, my God." He couldn't stop staring at the screen.

"Hey, Gabe, chill, man. Larry didn't think it was that bad."

Gabe managed a weak smile, not about to tell them why he was shaken. "Maybe not from your viewpoint, but you're not paying the lawyers to defend you."

"You got that right."

After the news segment finished and the others left, Gabe got the videotape out and played it again and again, freezing the frame when Emily turned sideways to get into her car.

Yes, she was most definitely pregnant. And she hadn't said a word to him in all the months they'd been e-mailing each other back and forth.

Maybe she thought he wouldn't be interested because it wasn't his child, but Gabe found he didn't care.

Suddenly, more than anything, more even than this project, he wanted to be with Emily. He didn't care that she wasn't having his baby, he loved her and he'd love her baby, too. She needed him now, no matter what she thought.

And this time he wasn't going to let her down.

She'd made the national news. With a sick feeling, Emily saw her pregnant self clearly silhouetted against the car. She held out a slim hope that Gabe hadn't seen the broadcast.

That hope was dashed when he started calling the next morning. He'd seen it. He knew she was pregnant. What did he think? Was he angry? Hurt?

Happy?

Emily couldn't talk to him here, not at the office. Besides, she was truly busy and needed to concentrate.

Somehow, she made it through the day. When she got home, her answering machine was blinking like crazy.

And there was e-mail from Gabe.

I want to see you.

Well, she didn't want to see him. Emily listened to the six messages he'd left for her on her answering machine. They said basically the same thing, except for an ominous last one.

"If you won't come to me, then I'll come to you."

Ha. An empty threat. He couldn't come to her without jeopardizing the project. Still, she supposed she'd better e-mail him some sort of response.

Before she could do so, there were three more e-mails waiting from him.

One way or another, I am going to see you, the last one said.

Oh, great. Just great.

It looked like she was going to Arizona.

The biosphere reminded Emily of her stomach—large and round.

At least this time, she knew the drill, so she brought a hairdryer and a full set of makeup. They'd have to be irradiated and then blasted with ultrasonics and Emily wondered just what colors of makeup she'd get back.

"Uh, ma'am?" A young man's voice sounded outside the dressing room.

"Yes?"

"Sorry, ma'am, but we're having a hard time finding a space suit to fit you."

"Are you talking about those white jumpsuits? They were plenty baggy last time I was here."

"Gabe wants to see you in person, so you have to wear a space suit."

"A real space suit?" They were carrying this a little too far.

"Pretty real."

"And I suppose there aren't any maternity space suits."

The young man laughed. "Not yet, ma'am."

"Okay. Fine. See what you can do." At least she had time to do a good job on her hair and makeup.

However, it also gave her time to think and get anxious. Gabe was going to be so angry. She didn't want him angry, but could she blame him?

*   *   *

Gabe was impatient and the space suit was hot. The internal temperature control wasn't working right, which was why they'd been red-tagged. But they were fine for short-term use, the key being *short*-term.

Where was Emily? Gabe paced, which didn't help the temperature inside the suit any.

After half an hour, he'd convinced himself that she'd changed her mind.

After forty-five minutes, he'd had enough waiting. And he didn't want to talk to Emily through a space helmet, he wanted to hold her in his arms.

He wanted to hold her in his arms more than anything.

Anything.

The suit they found for Emily had been made for a man who was six feet five inches tall, and was bulky enough so that a seven-months-pregnant woman could squeeze her way inside and have a foot of extra arm and leg material to fight with.

Why had she bothered with her hair and makeup?

Just how unalluring could a human being be?

Emily finally made it to the visitor's room. Gabe was already there, standing silently, looking at the photographs of the biosphere in various phases of construction that were hung on the wall.

He didn't even acknowledge her presence. This was going to be harder than she thought. "Gabe, I know you're angry, but please, hear me out."

The figure didn't move.

Great. He was so angry he wouldn't even look at her.

"I love you. I always have. And I can't stop. I've tried and tried and I just wanted a part of you all to myself. I know I should have told you about the baby, but I was afraid, afraid that either you wouldn't care, or you'd only be interested in the baby and not me. And then, and then how could you see our baby and not want to hold it? I just didn't know what to do!"

Still the figure didn't move.

Emily started crying. "Gabe, say something!"

A door opened. "Hello, Em."

Gabe's voice came from behind her. Emily turned and saw him standing there in the doorway. He was wearing slacks and a shirt and there was no sign of a space suit or even the white jumpsuit.

Then who had she been talking to? Emily walked forward and lifted the reflective visor of the space-suited figure's helmet and saw a mannequin inside.

She'd just confessed her love to a dummy.

She eyed Gabe speculatively and hoped she wasn't starting a trend. "Wait a minute—if one of us gets to wear regular clothes, then it should be me, not you. What is up with you people?"

Gabe just smiled and walked over to her, placing his hands on her stomach. "Oh, Em."

Feeling the pressure of his hands on her stomach, even through the layers of material, made tears trickle down her cheeks.

"Don't cry." He helped her off with her helmet.

"You can't do this, can you?" she asked when her head was free.

"I can do anything I want to."

"But—"

"Hush." And he kissed her, a sweet, unhurried kiss. "What are you wearing under this?"

"One of those fashionable white jumpsuits."

"Okay, then let's get this thing off."

"But, Gabe, what about—"

He interrupted her again with a quick kiss. "Doesn't matter anymore."

"Why? What happened? Gabe, don't tell me you settled with those opportunistic vultures. *Please* tell me you didn't kill the project."

"I didn't and I won't. They don't have a case. I hired your company and that's that." He worked on the fasteners on the space suit.

"I know what the contract says, I wrote it. They know it, too, but they're trying to get the public on their side."

"Don't worry about it," he said when that's all she'd been doing for forty-eight hours. "The public's children are fascinated with their plants, remember Christmas?"

Did she. EduPlaytion had had their best ever year. Emily had earned a sizable bonus that she'd already earmarked for a beginning college fund.

"Those toys are still selling and Christmas was a month ago," Gabe said. "Okay, let's get you out of this thing. I'm not proposing to a woman in a space suit."

Proposing? Emily froze. "Gabe—"

He kissed her.

"You keep interrupting me."

"Because you keep talking. Just listen." He started pulling the top of the suit off her arms. "I love you. I never stopped. And I'll love your baby, too, Em. I want to help you raise it and be a father to it. It doesn't matter that I'm not the biological father. I'll be a father in every other way that counts."

"Oh, Gabe." Emily started crying then, great gulping sobs.

He pulled the last of the suit off and she clung to him, sobbing. He was going to hate her. He was going to hate her so much.

And she had to tell him anyway. "Gabe," she managed with a little catch in her voice. Taking his hands she put them on her stomach.

Just then, the baby gave a great kick. Seeing the wonder on Gabe's face made her start crying all over again.

"Did it hurt?"

"No, no."

"But Emily, you're supposed to be happy."

"Gabe, it's your baby!" she blurted out.

"Mine? You mean we…?"

In answer, Emily nodded and continued to cry.

"It's our baby? Yours and mine?"

"Ye-es," she sobbed.

She was carrying his child and all the months they'd shared their opinions, their feelings and their dreams, she'd never said a word. She hadn't even told him she was pregnant at all.

Reaction set in. He'd thought they were true soul mates. He'd come to realize that their love was a rare and precious thing and they'd both been too young to manage such a powerful force. Now, they were older and more experienced and the love had waited until they were ready for it.

And in spite of this love, she'd never told him that she was undergoing the most profound experience of a woman's life, let alone experiencing it with *his* child.

From deep within him came the agonized question, "Why didn't you tell me?"

Emily, sobbing quietly now, just shook her head.

But she didn't have to answer because as soon as the words left Gabe's mouth, he knew the answer.

Because she knew she couldn't count on him, that's why she hadn't told him. He'd walked out once. No, he'd walked out twice.

"I wanted to tell you," she said in a whisper. "And I already told the stupid dummy over there…but you were in the biosphere and your e-mails were so wonderful. You were talking to me, not because I was pregnant, but just for me. I let too much time go by and…"

"Never mind. I'm here now. And I've changed. Truly I have, Em."

"I don't want you to change—I just want you around and your baby will want you around, too. So, I'll bring him or her to visit as often as I can, but when you get out of this thing, I want your promise that no matter what the project or how good, or how important it is, you only work on one that allows you to come home to us at night."

"Okay." She was talking like they had a future together. His heart picked up speed.

"Gabe, I'm completely serious."

"So am I."

"If you want to be a part of this child's life, then you have to be there for everything—music lessons, school plays, Scouts, birthdays, Christmas—all of it."

"I intend to."

She looked at him doubtfully. He could hardly blame her. "You don't believe me, do you?" he asked.

"I want to believe you."

Smiling, Gabe took her hand and led her to the door of the meeting room.

Then he opened it.

Emily gasped. "Gabe! What are you doing? You aren't supposed to leave the room!"

"I'm getting your clothes from the decontamination area. Fetching as that white jumpsuit is, I'm sure you'll want to get married in something else." He smiled at her. "Meet you back here in ten minutes."

"But—"

He kissed her again. "No more talking."

Gabe went back to the visitor's room, this time on the other side of the glass.

Marta Elkins burst through the door on the biosphere side about two minutes before Gabe expected her.

"What are you doing out there! I heard—"

"You mean you spied."

She didn't bother to deny it. "You've compromised the project."

"No, I've just compromised me. Congratulations, Marta." Gabe removed his security tag and tossed it on the table. "You're now in charge. Have fun."

"I don't believe this, although I should have expected it. You lack the formal academic training and the discipline for a project of this scope."

Gabe stood. "You forget. I conceived this project. I designed the experiments. My company raised the funds that built this project. I am this project. You'll still report to me." With a casual salute, he walked back to the decontamination area.

Emily was waiting for him. Without a word, he took her hand and opened the door that led to the outside foyer.

"Gabe!" What was he doing?

He kept walking until they were standing outside in the open air.

"What have you done?"

He took a deep breath and smiled. "Walked out."

"You can't do that."

"I just did. Hey, how about a steak? I haven't had meat in months. I'll bet junior, there, would like a steak."

He'd left a project. Gabe had actually walked out on a project. "I can't let you jeopardize all the biosphere experiments—what about the people who need food?"

"They're not going to be growing it in a controlled environment, are they? No, they'll have to contend with wind and bugs and hail and smog. I should have had a control farm going beside each of the biospheres, but I ran out of time and money. Now, I've got the time—and since the toys were such a hit, I'll bet EduPlaytion has got the money."

He took her in his arms. "There'll be other opportunities, but I know there won't be any other opportunities with you. I came real close to missing this one, Em. I'm not taking any more chances."

Emily felt the happiness grow within her until there wasn't room for so much happiness and a baby both. "No regrets?"

"I'd be lying if I said I won't have a twinge or two sometimes."

"Listen, mister. You know nothing about twinges. Let me tell you about twinges."

"Can you tell me over a steak?"

"I can tell you over rotten banana peels. We're talking *serious* twinges."

They walked toward the car Emily had rented.

"Did I mention the part about us getting married?"

Emily grinned. "I did hear the word in passing."

"You will marry me again, won't you, Em?"

"Yes," she said, consideringly. "And I think the sooner, the better."

"That's what I was thinking."

Gabe opened the door for her and Emily was more than happy to let him drive.

"So where are we going to eat?" she asked.

"Nevada."

"Gabe?"

"You said the sooner we're married, the better."

"Yes, but—"

He leaned over and kissed her. "You've just got to learn when to stop talking."

Emily grinned. "I already know. I just like being kissed."

EPILOGUE

"I'VE never seen such gorgeous flowers!" The organist at the Starlite Wedding Chapel in Nevada admired Emily's bouquet.

Gabe had stopped at three florists before he was satisfied with the flowers. They were all in white, a profusion of roses, baby's breath, gardenias and orchids.

Emily had a wreath of white rosebuds in her hair and was wearing a soft silk pantsuit in turquoise.

They were alone for this wedding, except for the justice of the peace and the organist, and Emily decided she liked it better than before.

This time, it was just two of them—well, three of them—declaring their love and vowing to have a future together.

"I now pronounce you husband and wife—or should I say family?" the J.P. declared, having been told that this was Gabe and Emily's second trip to the altar.

As Gabe drew her into his arms for their kiss, he whispered, "Family. I like the sound of that."

And Emily whispered back, "So do I."

You're not going to believe this offer!

**In October and November 2000, buy any two Harlequin
or Silhouette books and save $10.00 off future purchases,
or buy any three and save $20.00 off future purchases!**

Just fill out this form and attach 2 proofs of purchase (cash register
receipts) from October and November 2000 books and Harlequin will
send you a coupon booklet worth a total savings of $10.00 off future
purchases of Harlequin and Silhouette books in 2001. Send us 3 proofs
of purchase and we will send you a coupon booklet worth a total
savings of $20.00 off future purchases.

Saving money has never been this easy.

I accept your offer! Please send me a coupon booklet:

Name: _____

Address: _____ City: _____

State/Prov.: _____ Zip/Postal Code: _____

Optional Survey!

In a typical month, how many Harlequin or Silhouette books would you buy <u>new</u> at retail stores?

☐ Less than 1 ☐ 1 ☐ 2 ☐ 3 to 4 ☐ 5+

Which of the following statements best describes how you <u>buy</u> Harlequin or Silhouette books?
Choose one answer only that <u>best</u> describes you.

☐ I am a regular buyer and reader

☐ I am a regular reader but buy only occasionally

☐ I only buy and read for specific times of the year, e.g. vacations

☐ I subscribe through Reader Service but also buy at retail stores

☐ I mainly borrow and buy only occasionally

☐ I am an occasional buyer and reader

Which of the following statements best describes how you <u>choose</u> the Harlequin and Silhouette
series books you buy <u>new</u> at retail stores? By "series," we mean books within a particular line,
such as *Harlequin PRESENTS* or *Silhouette SPECIAL EDITION*. Choose one answer only that
<u>best</u> describes you.

☐ I only buy books from my favorite series

☐ I generally buy books from my favorite series but also buy
books from other series on occasion

☐ I buy some books from my favorite series but also buy from
many other series regularly

☐ I buy all types of books depending on my mood and what
I find interesting and have no favorite series

Please send this form, along with your cash register receipts as proofs of purchase, to:
In the U.S.: Harlequin Books, P.O. Box 9057, Buffalo, NY 14269
In Canada: Harlequin Books, P.O. Box 622, Fort Erie, Ontario L2A 5X3
(Allow 4-6 weeks for delivery) Offer expires December 31, 2000.

PHQ4002

Romance is just one click away!

love scopes

- Find out all about your guy in the Men of the Zodiac area.
- Get your daily horoscope.
- Take a look at our Passionscopes, Lovescopes, Birthday Scopes and more!

join Heart-to-Heart, our interactive community

- Talk with Harlequin authors!
- Meet other readers and chat with other members.
- Join the discussion forums and post messages on our message boards.

romantic ideas

- Get scrumptious meal ideas in the Romantic Recipes area!
- Check out the Daily Love Dose to get romantic ideas and suggestions.

Visit us online at

www.eHarlequin.com

on Women.com Networks

Duets™

Presenting...

HARLEQUIN®

REGENCY ROMANCE

Experience the opulence of the era captured vividly in these novels. Visit elegant country manors, town houses and the English countryside and explore the whirlwind of social engagements that London "Society" revolved around. Embark on captivating adventures with the feisty heroines who unintentionally tame the roguish heroes with their wit, zest and feminine charm!

All she wants is a baby!

Popular Harlequin Romance® author,

Heather MacAllister,

invites you to share
Emily's and Freddie's baby fever!

They're best friends who've been too busy with
their careers to have babies. But now both of
them are ready to get pregnant at last....

Will their pregnancy project succeed?

Find out what happens in:

THE PATERNITY PLAN (#3625)
in October 2000

THE MOTHERHOOD CAMPAIGN (#3629)
in November 2000

*Available in October and November
wherever Harlequin books are sold.*

HARLEQUIN®
Makes any time special.™

Visit us at www.eHarlequin.com   HRPREG